A Battleaxe and a Metal Arm 6:

Cannibal Dining Room

Samuel Fleming

Cover Art by David Leahey

ISBN-13: 978-1-954679-17-7 (paperback)
ISBN-13: 978-1-954679-16-0 (ebook)

Thank you to my Beta Readers

and to my First Reader,

Mel.

iv

Contents

"There are many ways to
suffer. Death is one of the
least painful."
—forgotten

Previously...

Helesys and Taunauk had journeyed far. After awaking in the dungeon for the first time, they journeyed through the flooded realm of the fishmen. There they fought and skulked their way through the depths, through the rusted prison and the temple. They met the unfortunate creature, Pitiful Lull, and rescued a water elemental by pulling a metal plate from its water body. They ultimately perished by the maws of the giant hydra, but were reborn in the same hallway—or so they thought. Two things changed: The hallway was different, and the heroes had returned with the metal wolf-plate, bringing the treasure with them across the realms and beyond death.

In the second realm, they found the barracks of the dungeon inhabited by goblins who followed the god, Zhug. After fleeing into the crypts, Taunauk nearly perished at the grasp of Shomosk, the many-handed horror. Above, they were accosted by obsidian mechanical soldiers. Even though they fought valiantly and Taunauk glowed golden with unrealized power, the wounded Taunauk and Helesys were ultimately taken prisoner and brought before the goblin god. It was in Zhug's throne room they learned Zhug was not a god, but a giant of staggering size and intellect, with a treasure horde that afforded him enormous power. The heroes told him of their journey and how they brought back the wolf-plate after death—it was this fact that endeared them to Zhug, and he bestowed upon them a gift of their choosing before killing them and sending them wandering the realms. Helesys chose the magekiller token and Taunauk chose Everfall, the ironwood shield.

In their third rebirth, the heroes entered the wode, a dark and sprawling forest. There they met many inhabitants, including the wolf druids, led by Matron Mildé, and the village ruled over by the Deacon. The Deacon's village was especially troubling, as the channeler used the flesh of his people to make things for them—tools, homes, even children. Ultimately, Helesys came to despise both the Matron and the Deacon for choosing to rule and stagnate, rather than try to escape. Their journey led them to a crumbling Gatehouse, where the Green Knight told them the story of the Gatekeeper and her Wolf-Knight—the first hints of who the heroes needed to seek if they were to escape. Wielding the magic of the grove and her own imbued weapons, the Green Knight slew Taunauk before Helesys could end defeat the Knight. Weary, Helesys wandered the wode until she found and climbed the infinite wall—doomed to fall to her death.

Thankfully, Helesys and Taunauk were reborn together again in the hallway. This time, their journey led them underground, through a giant borehole and into the path of the greatworm and the giant lizard. After avoiding the first and besting the second, the heroes found themselves in a giant insect hive. They fought a magic wielding scion and a heavily armored guard, then ran into slaves of varying species—including Terrans. In the depths they came upon the insect queen, who threatened to make the heroes into slaves. As they left, Helesys slaughtered two dozen Terran slaves—their death giving them freedom to wander. In retaliation, the queen sent Paraxnae, the spider-king, after them. To defeat its terrible speed and ferocity, Helesys dug deep with her power and Taunauk channeled his golden glow—something only done a handful of times. Their journey deeper took them over a perilous underground chasm and nearly to their deaths at the tentacles of the beast below. At the ends of the realm, they came upon the glassmen—strange beings who would not aid the heroes, and sent them wandering once again.

In the fifth instance, the oppressive halls of the dungeon gave way to stairs, and Helesys and Taunauk climbed upwards for the first time since their imprisonment. They saw hanging banners and carvings of the wolves, the symbols that seemed to haunt the dungeon, before they encountered the first resistance: Firebreathing stone men and guard drakes. Helesys tried to suppress the stone men's fire, but they were made-things and bolstered against such magic.

The weaver and barbarian eventually slew the lizards and destroyed the stone men with the help of a mysterious new ally, Shawn. A man of dark dress and airy mood, he accompanied the heroes up the final flights of the stairs. Careful not to fall behind and succumb to whatever horrors stalked them from below.

At the top of the stairs they came to a locked iron door, with a key slot made for the wolf-plate—for the relic that Helesys had been holding on to since the flooded temple. Beyond the door lay a greenhouse that stretched into a vast forest. They avoided the arbormen and a giant golden deer, and fought off a group of burrowing landsharks. Shawn displayed an aptitude with his blades and proved to be a cunning ally once again.

Their journey brought them to an ash and frost-covered swath of hills. They pressed into the center, into the middle of the swirling frost, but Shawn succumbed to the cold magic and

Taunauk turned back with their newfound comrade. Helesys pressed forward and at the center found the skeletal remnants of a battle between two mages. On the finger of one, sat a ring a frost. Helesys removed the ring and place it on her mundane hand, taking the relic for herself.

The trio journeyed on toward a black tower that rose over the trees and to the glass ceiling in the sky. Inside, they found a massive platform that would lock them in and raise them up to the roof of the greenhouse. But inside they were accosted by ghoulish shades and then by the dancer—a long-limbed fiend with claws that could reach clear across the room. Again, Helesys felt her magic weak against the bolstered creature, but she reached out with a holding spell.

It was then that she came face to face with the creature's mind before Taunauk slew it. She saw a mind both blank and vicious, and a reflection of Helesys's own mind—of some dark, hidden depth.

The black tower brought them to the ramparts. Across the roof loomed a tower, but they had to escape the wrath of a giant dragon. Helesys was forced to use both her wand-arm and her newfound ring of frost to assault the dragon, but each use of the ring of frost came with great pain. Worse, Shawn was painfully affected by the cold magic of the relic, and ran off across the roof to pick the locked door to the tower. The trio managed to outrun the dragon and enter the safety of the tower.

Inside, they found the old mage, Amadeus, who revealed that he had been following their progress through his realm and recognized the Everfall shield that Taunauk carried. Shawn revealed he was like the other two—that he could also bring back relics.

Their new ally answered many questions, chief of which revealed that the dungeon was a soul trap, a bottomless well from which souls cannot escape. The only chance lay at the mercy of the Wolf-King, the ruler of the dungeon and a mage so powerful that neither Amadeus nor Zhug would face him.

When their questions turned to the Gatekeeper, the lady and love of the Wolf-King, Amadeus shrank from their questions. The Wolf-King possessed him, reaching through all the wards of the mage's sanctum. Helesys, Taunauk and Shawn, struggled to stand against the might of the controlled mage and were ultimately forced to jump out of the tower window rather than risk lingering injury at the unknowable assault of magic.

The three fell to their deaths, but only Helesys and Taunauk woke up together in that same starting room. They were left with more questions, many revolving around their new comrade. How was it that Shawn could bring things back, but wasn't reborn with them? Would they see him again?

Neither Helesys nor Taunauk felt that they had seen the last of Shawn.

~ ~ ~

The Dining Room

Taunauk went first down the hallway. Helesys followed.

The barbarian walked with torch in hand. His massive shoulders and fur collar of his cloak cast a deep shadow on his opposite side. The spellweaver walked behind him, half-illuminated. Torchlight flickered sharply off her metal hand, casting bright pinpricks of starlight on the stone beside her waist.

The stones extended out into the darkness in front and behind them to the limits of the torchlight, and then the darkness stretched on for miles in either direction—seemingly endless.

Their bootsteps echoed quietly on the stone.

How quaint they must look at first glance, Helesys thought. *Capable, yet quaint.*

Taunauk was a giant of a human. An equally large battleaxe and wooden shield hung on his backslings. A look of fierce certainty always on his face. His hair and beard sliced to utilitarian stubble. If one looked deeper, they would see that his cloak hid the mountain of coiled muscles of his shoulders and arms. The shield was ironwood, stronger than steel. His battleaxe was worn pale at the grips, and the twin blades were chipped from countless years of battle.

If one were foolish enough to cross him, then they would learn that his Everfall shield was magical. That his axe was as quick and deadly as a thunderstrike and that he was a true barbarian. One-who-fights-beyond-death. They might even see that he was more—that some other magic or power flowed within him. Something that caused him to glow a golden orange in desperate times of need—times when even the rage of an Endroggen barbarian wasn't enough.

Helesys was an elf, taller than most humans, yet not her comrade. Her skin was noble-fair. Her white hair was cropped short, yet made to look shoulder length with minor magic. The cloak hid much of her and was a simple thing compared to her armor underneath.

The dungeon had stolen much of their memories, but Helesys did remember a noble house. It was a memory that explained her appearance, at least in part.

But she also remembered blastshells and a battlefield.

Underneath her cloak, Helesys wore elven chainmail which hung light as silk on her shoulders. She had the poise and dexterity of a soldier… And the practiced violence of one as well. Then there was her metal arm. Prosthetic from shoulder to fingertips. It looked like a gauntlet at first glance; the same mithral as her chainmail. Yet underneath it was a mix of clockwork and arcane power, made to harness the magic wand embedded in the center of her forearm.

It was more than a weapon—it was an extension of herself. Helesys felt every trickle and surge of power, yet she could also feel through the metal as if it were skin. She ran her metal fingertips over the wall as she walked and felt the cold and the roughness of the stone.

Sometimes she could almost pretend that her arm was real. Only the scraping of her metal on the stone ruined the illusion.

"Do you sense something?" Taunauk asked, pausing his stride.

Helesys pulled her metal hand away from the wall. "No. It is nothing. Just *feeling the stone*."

"Oh."

Taunauk turned and kept walking, but Helesys saw the quick look of embarrassment on his face.

"It is okay. I forget sometimes that the arm isn't my own." She clasped her hands together, and felt warm skin against one and cold metal against the other.

"It is possible to forget a great many things, simply by not thinking of them."

Helesys thought on this a moment, then shook her head. "Did you make that up just now?"

The barbarian chuckled in the gloom, and Helesys shared a small smile.

It was as lighthearted a moment as they could find here in the dungeon or castle… Helesys would always think of it as a dungeon and a prison, no matter how it looked from afar. The wizard, Amadeus, had divulged that the place was a *soul trap*, a well that souls fell into and could never escape. This was why, even in death, a soul did not go to an afterlife. After dying, they awoke in the dungeon, again and again, in a different part of the dungeon every time.

The drowned temple, the abandoned barracks, the ancient forest, the buried hive, then in the tower of the old wizard, Amadeus. Five times they had died and been reborn.

At least Helesys and Taunauk were growing used to each other's company.

The first time they appeared together, they had looked at each with apprehension and the faintest echo of remembrance. Their first steps had been tentative. Measured. But each time they were reborn together, that apprehension had faded. They relearned strategies for fighting. Even relearning a shared humor.

There were things about them that one could not easily discern. The magic that belied Helesys's arm. Taunauk's golden glow under duress. The struggles that they had been through over these five deaths…

Helesys's metal hand brushed the cold stone of the hallway again, bringing her mind back from wandering and to the oppressive reality through which they walked.

~

They were getting toward the end. Fog rolled into the hallway, rolling past their shins and not quite covering the stone. They walked deeper and deeper into it and soon could not see more than a few hundred feet in front of or behind them. Eventually, the cool mist clung to Helesys's face and hair.

Taunauk walked with Everfall shield and torch in hand. Helesys kindled her wand-arm, if only for reassurance. The two walked in an uneasy silence.

Miles later, the hallway ended.

Green ferns and stalks pierced the veil between the gray light of mist and dusk. Underbrush and dead leaves crackled beneath their feet. The chirps and squawks of birds filtered through the mist. The scene looked as though it belonged to a jungle.

Taunauk grunted in dissatisfaction and stepped cautiously into the gloom.

"What's the matter?" Helesys asked, following.

"Mist."

When the barbarian didn't elaborate further, she prodded. "What's wrong with it, other than not being able to see danger clearly?"

"It's cold and wet. It gets everywhere. *And* you can't see danger clearly."

Helesys smirked, the humor a small release of tension. "Do you think the hallway…"

The elf turned and saw that the stones that marked the hallway were already gone. It had only been a few steps away. Now it was nothing more than empty air. She walked back and ran her metal hand over where the entrance *should be*, but found nothing. No hidden stones, no remnants of magic. Nothing but mist.

She turned back to Taunauk. "I'm beginning to think that is a trick of the dungeon or the Wolf-King, and that they don't like us retracing our steps."

"They are herding us." Taunauk said the words matter-of-factly. He cast the torch aside, no longer needing it in the perpetual gray light, and drew his giant battleaxe.

"Herding us to where? To what end?"

"To death—the same end we always meet." He turned and studied his comrade. "Does that trouble you?"

Helesys met his eyes. "No. The act doesn't bother me. The reasoning behind it gives me pause."

"You assume there is reason behind it. Most creatures do not act on reason. Most Terrans don't either."

They shared a gallow's smirk. Helesys said, "On that we can agree."

~

Helesys and Taunauk pressed deeper into the jungle. Jagged, broad-leafed plants seemed to pierce through the mist, like pointed fingers reaching through the veil. Rotting leaves littered the ground and made it impossible to be completely silent as they walked. Wispy trees disappeared into the gray above. In every direction they looked it was much the same—sight, sounds, smell, feel all seemed to blur together in the haze—obscuring any sense of direction or progress.

They happened upon the first truly massive tree, nearly twenty feet wide. The bark was the color of clay, smooth, and appeared almost like a polished column at a glance. It was carved with deep geometric patterns that wrapped all the way around the trunk and disappeared into the mist—no telling how far up they went.

Helesys examined the tree, noting the circles, diamond patterns, and interlocking lines. "Impossibly neat," she mumbled, pointing not just to the straight lines and smooth curves, but also to the evenness of the grooves.

"Magic?" Taunauk asked. He glanced at the patterns on the tree, but kept his focus on the surrounding mist.

"Has to be." She ran her metal hand over the grooved designs but felt nothing. "No Terran hand could've made carvings so perfect. But whatever magic made these is long gone. Lost deep in time."

Helesys guessed that they had gone a quarter mile before they came to another equally large, carved tree.

Helesys examined the design. "The same or nearly so."

"What does this mean?" Taunauk asked, speaking of the trees.

The weaver shook her head. "I do not know."

This time, a shiver ran down her neck. Helesys scanned the mist, gauntlet whirring quietly with readiness and power.

Taunauk turned, the leather grips of his axe handle squeezing beneath his grip.

The mist lingered. Empty. Silent save for an absent squawk of a distant parrot. Nothing came for them.

"Come," Taunauk said quietly. "Let us not dwell on ghosts."

Helesys followed him, her gaze following the grooves as they walked around the tree's girth.

"Wait," she said, pausing mid-step.

Taunauk turned and walked over.

In front of her were more carvings. This time they were freshly gashed; ghostly-white inner bark and dried sap shown through. This time, letters were scrawled.

The other grooves and designs in the bark were clay-colored and old. However, those larger designs had been made, it happened so long ago that the tree had healed back to its original clay color. The magic that made the grooves was gone, and likely too was the mage who commanded it. She thought again of the Deacon's words, of the dungeon grinding even gods to dust. No one could survive the cycle of deep time and endless rebirth. Not for eternity.

The barbarian ran his fingers over the newer letters, discerning the sap and white inner bark. "Half a day old at most. Can you read it?"

Helesys ran her metal hand over the surface, but neither she nor her wand recognized them. She shook her head and replied, "No, but it appears that not everyone is long gone."

~

Helesys followed Taunauk through the fern-laden under-brush, wand-arm churning quietly with readied power.

She cursed the dead leaves and brush that crunched beneath her feet. The birds high above the mist seemed content to an-nounce this as well, cawing and crowing as they passed beneath. She cursed them too and would've given much to move silently—especially since other Terrans might be nearby.

Helesys had forgotten much since waking in the dungeon—her spells a chief disappointment. She imagined that she knew a great many, but the words were lost to her. The few spells she did remember had come back to her in times of dire need or she had parsed from other weavers and channelers; using their knowledge for her own gain.

The spellweaver searched her mind, hoping that some for-gotten spell of silence would return to her, but this time neither her memory nor wand were merciful.

Another mile into the forest, Taunauk stopped suddenly and pointed off into the mist.

There were three Terran faces half-hidden behind mist and ferns. Helesys would've missed them, save for their bright red eyes that stood out like gemstones.

Helesys and Taunauk stared, and the faces stared back.

After a long moment, one of the terrans stepped forward cautiously. The human woman was light-skinned and wrapped messily in hides. Her white hair was short and sheared wildly. She wore stone and pearl jewelry around her neck, wrists and ankles—a nature-centric culture not unlike the wolf-druids of the wode...

She whispered something in a language that neither Helesys nor Taunauk understood. Helesys's wand-arm warmed with effort, trying to translate, but the spell failed. The woman took one of the bone necklaces off and presented it to Helesys. Helesys nodded wearily and took the offering. The shards of the necklace worn smooth, down to indistinguishable nubs and shafts, and strung together with thick cord. With her gauntlet, Helesys felt the faintest remnants of magic, like the smell of a long smoldered fire. Rather than put it around her neck, the weaver placed it in a pocket of her robe and nodded.

Then the woman motioned for them to follow.

Neither the barbarian nor the spellweaver took their eyes off the newcomers for a long moment. Then Taunauk turned to Helesys, just enough to keep the others in view. "What do you think?"

The weaver sighed. "I think that after the wolf-druids and the Deacon's village, I am hesitant to trust any Terrans. *But* it is better than wandering blindly through the jungle."

"Agreed."

~

Helesys and Taunauk walked abreast, following behind the natives—just close enough to keep view of them in the mist.

Along with the human woman, there was a small male goblin and a high-browed Terran with three fingers on each hand—a species that neither Helesys nor Taunauk recognized. They seemed to defer to the white-haired woman's path and orders.

All three of the natives stalked silently through the underbrush, and Helesys felt a pang of jealousy.

Sometime later, they came upon a deep gorge. Here the underbrush gave way to packed stone, and the mist swirled and parted, cut through by gusts that funneled through the ravine. The wind cleared a view of the gorge several hundred feet to the left or right. They could see across the chasm, some fifty feet, but could see no way to make it across or safely make it down the sheer wall. Nor could they see further across the other side as the mist continued past the rocks.

Down below, the mist swirled ominously, hiding both the depth of the drop and anything that might lurk below. Helesys thought of the perilous rock bridge that they had crossed beneath the buried hive and the tentacled monstrosity that had lurked in the darkness below it. The more she lingered on the image, it wasn't the thought of a monster lurking in those dark corners that troubled her; it was that in every corner of the dungeon, there was something trapped, something trying to live a meager existence—be it Terran, god or monster. Every corner of this bottled world, filled with something just as trapped as they.

The white-haired woman eyed Helesys and Taunauk and brought a closed fist to her mouth—a symbol for silence. The three natives turned together and walked parallel to the gorge. Helesys and Taunauk followed.

Eventually, they came to a fallen tree that spanned the gorge—one of the massive, carved ones. Even though the width of it was half sunk in the ground, the bulk of it still towered over their heads. Now they could see the carvings in earnest, that the geometric wrappings spanned the entire length of the barkless tree, disappearing into mist on either end. Helesys studied the patterns, searching for a larger picture or writing on its surface, but could see nothing; there seemed no logic to the circles, diamonds and interlocking lines. Only that the markings on each of these special trees seemed identical to her eye.

Meanwhile, the human tribeswoman began to climb up the side of the tree, using the grooves of the design as handholds and footholds. The goblin and the three-fingered Terran followed. They waited wordlessly for Helesys and Taunauk to follow.

The comrades shared an uneasy glance and then followed. Taunauk made the climb in three lumbering steps. Helesys was reminded of her ill-fated climb up the infinite wall, the exhausting and unending climb. When she reached the top of the fallen trunk, she looked out over the mist and, for the briefest moment, imagined that she was standing atop the conquered wall and looking out over the wode—quickly savored and as quickly discarded.

The tribespeople led them across the bridge of the fallen tree. Rather than keep their arms down or outstretched for balance, they walked with arms folded their chests—a pose that reminded Helesys of a corpse being laid to rest. Crossing was a slow, measured affair and it was not apparent why—the fallen tree was wide enough and still enough that there was little danger of a misplaced step.

Halfway across, the mist below began to take shape. The amorphous swirling coalesced into Terran forms that pawed at the sides of the fallen tree. Their outline was little more than clouds and there were no eyes or mouth, nothing save for the vague Terran outline. They drifted across from the right side of the gorge, flowing as if caught in a ghostly river—most disappearing under the bridge. But not all. Some grasped the grooves of the tree and climbed up the sides, reaching in upward in slow, listless climbs.

Reaching toward the living.

Helesys kindled her wand-arm, ready should the mist get too close.

Taunauk said, "What devilry is this?"

The tribespeople stopped on the middle of the bridge and the lead woman turned. She said something in their native tongue, stooped down to a crouch, and reached out toward the closest mist spirit. It reached toward her, its ghostly hand about to grasp her. She waved a dismissive hand through the mist spirit's arm and head, scattering it as if it were no more than smoke.

The tribeswoman stood and turned impatiently, crossed her arms and kept walking.

Taunauk grumbled and followed, but Helesys lingered for one moment longer. It was just enough to confirm her suspicions: In their pause, she noticed that the mist spirits only clambered toward and reached out for the tribespeople. None had reached toward herself or Taunauk.

When they were safely across, Helesys whispered, "The mist has an eye for our guides."

The two leapt down from the make-shift bridge. Taunauk landed heavy on the ground and grumbled. Helesys leapt down and caught herself in a crouch on the grass.

The barbarian eyed the tribespeople and whispered, "The dead have minds and wills of their own. The living… they twist the truth to suit them. The dead do not lie, as the living do."

They followed the tribespeople into the veil of fog and the crunch of leaves. Helesys walked beside her comrade. She felt power and truth in his words—rather, that Taunauk *felt truth* in his words.

She asked, "Is that another echo of the past? Wisdom from a forgotten memory?"

The barbarian nodded, weariness in his eyes. "One still hidden away."

"You feel it is a burden," she said hesitantly.

After a long moment, he answered. "Yes."

Helesys thought back to his comments about the village—Taunauk felt he did not have such a village to return to—and to his deep longing at the green fields beneath the wizard's tower—that they were but a shadow of the barbarian fields of Endroggen, his home.

She nearly asked about Endroggen… but Taunauk looked as if he were a mountain on the brink of collapse, as if his eyes were holding back an avalanche.

Helesys placed a hand upon his towering shoulder. "If it is a burden, it is one we will bear together."

"We shall," he said and nodded reservedly.

Helesys's hand slipped from his shoulder and she felt that of the many hesitations in talking about their pasts. *This* was poignant for Taunauk. They were comrades, yet in that moment she felt *something* palpable dividing them. What burdens had they brought with them into this hellish place? What forgotten ghosts walked beside them?

~

They followed the tribespeople through the mist-covered forest for another mile before the mist suddenly broke.

Before them lay an unobstructed view of a jungle clearing and a village. Tents made of skin and hide littered the outskirts of the clearing. Dozens of other tribespeople milled about the tents, but suddenly jumped to silent attention as Helesys and Taunauk's group approached.

The entire clearing seemed to walk toward them, not in defense but in awe—with wide, red eyes. Even still, Helesys felt her wand gently hum to life. Taunauk reached upward for the pommel of his axe and this stalled most of the tribe. Those few that approached close enough to touch, did so slowly and reached out to the newcomers with bowed heads and barely touched them with fingertips.

Just beyond the group were stout guards with hide vests and bone clubs. It was only then that Helesys realized the strangeness of the tribe's dress: The hides they wore, the bone jewelry that adorned their ears and necks, and the bone weapons they carried...

Helesys whispered, "Taunauk, these things should disappear. Nothing dead stays in the realms." It was a clue that they had missed in the haste of their first deaths. They had not stayed to see the fishmen or Zhug's goblins... But all the subsequent deaths they'd witnessed had been followed by the bodies dissolving: The birchmen, the landsharks, Taunauk's own body in the wode.

Taunauk hummed, as if to confirm her suspicions.

Whispers rose from the village, none of which Helesys or her wand could understand—though she felt the wand in her arm tingle with effort.

Their guide, the human woman, reached out a hand toward them, then gestured for them to follow. The weaver and barbarian did so reluctantly. As they walked past the guards, Taunauk eyed their bone clubs. Each was a thick and formidable weapon, knobbed on either end.

"Do you see the bone clubs?" Taunauk asked, voice low. "They look like Terran thigh bones."

A shiver ran down Helesys's neck. She looked from the clubs to the other small bones that adorned the guards' ears and neck, but they were too small to make out.

"That is damning and disconcerting. Could they be from another creature? Perhaps a deer or a cow?" She did not know enough about anatomy to say either way.

Taunauk said nothing, and that was enough.

Helesys bolstered the energy in her gauntlet to a comforting, violent level. Meanwhile, the crowd of tribespeople still followed beside and behind them. The spellweaver wondered whether their reverence was a spiritual one or that of a baser—hungrier—urge.

Toward the middle of the clearing, they passed another of the massive, carved trees. The bottom was covered in slashed lettering—the same as they had passed in the forest. The rest of the carvings—the geometric patterns—rose up into the sky. This time, Helesys could see the whole of the massive structure. It was more tower than tree, a wooden cylinder that seemed to rise perfectly straight and uniform up to the limits of the mist.

In the center of the village clearing, a bonfire rose up. The pile of white logs and cinder rose up nearly twice the height of Taunauk, and billowed flames and pale smoke up to the limits of the mist; there the smoke and mist met and became indistinguishable. Even from afar, Helesys could feel the magic emanating from the fire—she reached her metal arm into the pocket of her robe, felt the bone necklace and confirmed her suspicion: The flames were a match to the smoldering remnants of magic of the bones.

As they crossed the final stretch of the clearing, Helesys felt the heat of the flames, even from fifty feet away and now saw the white logs for what they were—not bark of the great carved trees, but a massive pile of bones.

The villagers parted, leaving Helesys and Taunauk standing alone. In front of them, silhouetted by the roaring fire, stood three shamans. When Helesys's eyes adjusted, she saw they were wearing bone-covered garments; ribs were sewn around the midsection of their robes, broken slabs that might have been hips or shoulders were sewn onto the chest. Thin shards of bone dangled from the sleeves. Their faces were covered with skull masks, leaving only their mouths and chins. Each held a staff of the same bone white and lined with intricate carvings, but each was nearly as tall as the shaman and so they could not be Terran bone.

The murmuring of the village quieted until there was nothing but the crackling of fire.

Beside her, Taunauk stood with empty hands, but with a wide, ready stance—mirroring the churning power of her gauntlet.

The shamans stared, and the weaver and barbarian stared back. The moment grew heavy, as if the weight of the jungle mist was pressing down on them.

Heart pounding, and not sure what else to do, Helesys reached slowly for her knapsack. She dug for a ration of jerky. Then she took a bite of it, and tossed the silent crowd, who bit pieces off and passed them to the others.

"Meat," someone said. "Salty," said another. Helesys felt the quiet workings of translation within her arm and felt a quiet satisfaction that it was capable of learning.

The middle shaman, whose beard was woven into long braids, spoke. Helesys understood only snippets about "mist" and "jungle" while the wand struggled to decipher. Then the shaman's voice came through clearly.

"We give thanks," he said, with a wave of his staff, "for our brothers and sisters that have been taken by Logath. We leave the jungle in terror but are reborn. For each Logath takes, he gives us two more. By him, our numbers increase. By the sacred flame, they stay, blessing us with meat and bone. "

Then the shaman turned to the crowd of villagers. "Which offering shall we keep?"

While murmurs swept the crowd, Helesys mumbled, "This isn't looking good."

Taunauk grunted. "Did your wand tell you that?"

"I'm going to try something."

"You lead. I will follow."

Helesys raised her gauntlet above her head and let the sleeve slip down, revealing the metal of it, which glistened in the firelight. It glowed soft as the wand translated her words. "Logath has spoken to me." The village stilled as if the air had been sucked from the clearing. "We will not stay. We must speak to Logath. He demands it."

Her words shook both the villagers and the shamans. The latter whispered to each other, so that Helesys could not hear.

The main shaman raised his staff high overhead to silence the murmurs, then spoke. "Then *you* shall go to Logath. The large one shall stay as tribute to the loyal."

Taunauk reached overhead for his axe, but the shaman to the right, slender and three-fingered, called out, "*Tribidé undí*," and Taunauk froze just as he brought the axe down in front of him.

Though the wand in her arm didn't translate the language of spells, Helesys knew what it was: It was a holding spell that caused paralysis in the muscles. Right now, the shaman and Taunauk were having a psychic battle of wills; magic that Helesys had been on both sides of… and it was one that a fighter, even a barbarian, would have trouble winning against a weaver. Yet, Helesys heard the tightening of Taunauk's hands about the axe, and the slender shaman held the spell with teeth gritted.

Helesys leveled her gauntlet at the middle shaman and conjured power enough that purple lightning crackled and arced around her fingers. "He comes with me. You would deny the will of Logath?"

The shaman to the left, with elvish ears, sneered, "Deceiver!

Helesys heard footsteps behind her and turned to see four guards, bone clubs in hand. She spoke the words, "*Restu sonmovo, gardistoj*," but kept her barely contained blast leveled at the main shaman. The guards froze, mid-step—eyes wide in surprise.

In her mind, Helesys prepared for a psychic battle of wills. She'd used the holding spell against monsters and been forced to confront the equally distressing minds of the creatures. But now, the four men were just as frozen psychically as they were in reality. Helesys had expected a battle of wills against four men, but they might as well have been cowering like frightened children—it was no wonder that so many dark mages used the spell maliciously against non-weavers, for mundane people had no easy counter to it.

"Chantu, help me hold him," the three-fingered mage groaned. Her face was twisted into a grimace and Helesys could not help but smirk. She imagined the shaman and Taunauk in their own battle of wills where Taunauk was clawing his way closer and closer to his captor.

The elven mage, Chantu, spoke the same spell against Taunauk, "*Tribidé undí*," and the barbarian seemed frozen as if in a painting. The might of two mages was too much, even for a barbarian.

Helesys glared at the main shaman down the arcing metal of her gauntlet. He stood with bone staff in hand. His face was blank, but his eyes glanced around the scene, weighing the options.

Helesys did the same. Mental sequences unfurled before her. They were outnumbered both by guards and by weavers. Taunauk was more than a match for ten fighters, but Helesys doubted that she could repel the onslaught of three weavers, even inexperienced ones. To concentrate on multiple spells meant dividing her power… and risking being overpowered on any one front.

Her one chance would be a spreadfire blast, strong enough to kill the mages outright. She would lose her hold on the guards, but then Taunauk would be free.

She looked to either side of the shaman, to the villagers that were watching… to the villagers that were too close, too scared to move. Ten, maybe, that would be caught in the blast.

What was death in this endless realm, anyway? Even the death and pain of innocents?

"Do not be rash," the main shaman said. "You can still walk away."

Helesys glared back. "I will not leave him." There was a hollowness in her chest. Numbness. No, she would not leave her comrade here to be butchered and eaten, bones heaped upon the fire.

A brilliant, golden light flared beside them. Taunauk glowed as if he was set ablaze. Quiet orange flames flickered off his cloak, off his hair. His skin shimmered like molten metal. It was an inner, hidden power that neither Taunauk nor the weaver understood. One that her comrade channeled only in times of great need and only once in peace.

Taunauk moved, breaking the spell of two weavers—holding the massive battleaxe in front of him like a staff and resting the pommel on the ground. He spoke in overlapping voices, so many that Helesys could not count.

"We will not be bound against our will," the glowing barbarian said.

The center shaman stood, leaning wearily on his staff and dumbfounded at the impotence of their spell.

Then Taunauk turned to the three-fingered shaman, the one that had held him. *"Count yourself among the fortunate, for you have felt the rage of the Endroggen and lived to tell of it."* To the rest he said, "We are leaving in peace. To force our hand is to invite swift violence, and we shall feel no turmoil."

The elven shaman moved to speak but was quickly silenced by the elder. He nodded and said, quietly, "Go, both of you, for you are clearly blessed. Logath keep you." The glare in his eyes and the anger on the other shamans' faces told Helesys that it was no blessing.

Taunauk turned, and they walked through a silent, parting crowd. Helesys followed at his side. All the while, his glow did not cease, nor did Helesys cease the churning of power in her wand-arm. When they passed out of the clearing and back into the mist, Helesys ceased her hold on the guards; such was a weaver's strength over a commoner that she had nearly forgotten about them.

Helesys turned to her glowing companion, taking in the sight of him with growing questions; twice now, Taunauk had responded *"we"* when using this power. Both times the usage might have referred to herself, but something made her doubt.

And so Helesys asked, "To whom am I speaking?"

"You are speaking to Taunauk..." A moment later, the glow faded. "Why do you ask?"

Helesys shrugged. "It is a curious feat. I shall ask more of it when we are far from this place."

~ ~ ~

The Bonefield

Helesys and Taunauk pressed forward through the jungle mist without direction. They brushed aside thin-leaved ferns and only once more saw the carved trees.

Twice, they heard heavy footsteps in the mist. The weaver and barbarian paused, waiting with axe in hand and gauntlet humming with anticipation, but nothing leapt from the mist. Nothing came for them.

They passed a giant pitcher plant, nearly big enough to swallow Helesys's arm—a plant that hunted live prey by luring them in with sweet-smelling sap in the bottom of the pitcher. Flies buzzed inside, little more than shadows, and a quiet hum behind the plant's thick skin. Several flew vigorously, trying to escape back through the hole they had been lured through. One might escape, but most were trapped. Helesys thought of the dungeon and couldn't help but see the comparison—a cruel metaphor for their own plight.

Hours passed before the mist broke again and revealed a clearing. There were no ferns, no grass, no trees. The only thing growing from the dirt were rows and rows of small white seedlings, like a planter's field. Helesys searched the rows, each one growing steadily taller and taller… When the white plants were a foot high, she saw the knobs and points. Each wasn't a flowing plant, but a different bone: Lower legs, curved rib bones, the top of a skull, then whole rib cages, or folded legs. They reached out, rows of bones moving in sync, waving like white plants in a breeze.

Heavy footsteps behind them. They whipped around in time to see a giant's leg, splotchy gray and purple, disappear behind a spindly tree—far too thin a tree to hide a giant. Yet it was gone.

The barbarian stood squarely, axe in both hands, quiet determination on his face.

Helesys glanced from him to the trees, then to the trees all around, looking for movement. She whispered, "It's using magic to tree stride. That's how it's been following us—walking only a few steps at a time."

More movement behind them, across the bonefield.

Beyond the rows of single ribs and leg bones, beyond the skulls and rib cages, a half dozen creatures walked the fields: Twisted skeletons held together by tendons and sinew and only the faintest muscle. No skin hung from them. Only two were in the vaguest shape of Terran; one walked like a spider, splayed out on a mix of five legs and arms. Another had skulls for a torso and a ribcage for a head. Another with a skull inside flexing ribs.

They tended to the half-grown—to skeleton abominations that looked as if they were emerging from the dirt or had fallen into it at various angles. The bonemen rubbed and turned the embedded plants with care, with some motive and reason that Helesys couldn't imagine.

Taunauk whispered, "Foul magic works here."

Before Helesys could search for a way through the boneyard and past the skeletons, the sound of a crowd came from the fog and from the direction of the village. Again, Helesys and Taunauk turned to meet it.

A crowd of villagers emerged from the mist, led by the slender, three-fingered shaman. The subordinate who had first cast magic on Taunauk. The shaman smiled, teeth bared in a half-sneer, at the sight of her quarry. Three guards and three more men stood by her side. The latter were nothing more than villagers wielding bone clubs.

"I, Riona, have defied the will of the elders," she said, "to bring an end to the deceiver. You will not make it to Logath—"

Helesys called on her gauntlet and fired, catching the shaman by surprise. Riona and the nearby men dove to the ground as the purple blast tore past them. Several stayed on the ground, wide-eyed—but the shaman leapt to her feet.

Helesys fired two more times, but this time, the shaman stayed on her feet and managed to cast her spell. Riona shouted, *"Khutenri babalen reap!"* and scrawled a sigil with her staff.

The boneyard began to rattle. Each bone shook like a snake's tail and the clacks rose like deafening rain across the clearing.

Taunauk grumbled, "Take care of the weaver." He turned, not bothering to take the Everfall shield from his back—content with only the massive battleaxe—dividing his attention between the weaver and the boneyard. Through the field came the violent snaps of tendons and cracks of bone as a dozen skeleton creatures lumbered and skittered toward them.

"Tribidé lamara," said the shaman.

Helesys's muscles tightened, simultaneously contracting all at once and freezing her in place. Riona had cast the same paralysis spell on her that she had used on Taunauk earlier.

Even though the shaman was concentrating on the spell, somehow the boneyard still rattled with violence. She was either simultaneously concentrating on multiple spells—a feat not to be taken lightly—or she had called on some latent magic in this foul place.

The shaman and the weaver were locked in a psychic battle of wills. Even though Riona was across the field, flanked by men who had finally risen to their feet, Riona was also standing beside Helesys. She loomed over Helesys's shoulder, her breath so close Helesys could smell the meat and marrow that still lingered on her breath.

Across the field, Riona's face twisted into a grimace of struggle. "Attack!" she gasped. The men ran toward Helesys, some raising the bone clubs wildly overhead in their zealousness.

Before Helesys could break free—before she even felt the burning aid of the magekiller token—she felt her gauntlet move on its own. Her wand-arm raised and fired repeated blasts at the approaching men. The lot of them dove to the sides. Two weren't so lucky—half broken and half burst by the impact—sent sprawling backward.

Helesys felt the recoil of the blasts, but because she was paralyzed, she teetered and nearly fell. She fired three more silently screaming blasts of arcane energy directly at Riona. The shaman dove to avoid them.

Only then did she feel the magekiller token burn inside the metal of her arm, its blood-stained power cutting through the paralyzing magic of the shaman. A moment later, Helesys shook herself free from Riona's spell.

Behind her, the horrid snaps of tendons and shattering of bone continued. Taunauk was a blur of steel, swinging his battleaxe in wild, massive arcs. For the moment, he was only a barbarian. There was no golden glow of hidden power. Endroggen rage seemed more than match enough for the bone horde.

"Deceiver! Magekiller!" Riona shouted. "*Crebezon millizouvi.*"

A wave of energy pulsed from the shaman. Bugs crawled and buzzed from the ground. The small budding bones started to jump like frogs. They crawled, leapt and swarmed toward Helesys. The men that were still on their feet ran back toward their shaman, away from the creeping mass.

She leveled her gauntlet and fired toward the swarm. Each silent blast of arcane fire was punctuated by a thump as it slammed into the ground and threw dirt overhead. But still the swarm came, so thick it seemed to wash toward her like a flood.

Helesys grit her teeth and called on the ring of frost, "*Hieme murum.*" The crystal on her mundane finger glowed a sharp, brilliant blue. Flakes of frost swirled around her, conjured from the humid air. The weaver shivered the ring's energy pulsed from her—a painful trade that she had only called on once before and did not fully understand. The tendril of frost ran through her nerves. Down her legs, arms, feet, and fingertips. It slithered out and Helesys grimaced at the scraping sensation.

The tendril of frost flailed around her like a bullwhip, each snap sending a pulse of frost that brightened the bonefield like lightning. Bugs and bones were washed away by the blasts of power, but that did not stop the horde.

Across the field, the shaman screamed at her, but Helesys could not hear her from behind the veil of icy white.

Helesys willed the ring to conjure one great blast. She felt the words, the soft voice of the ring, *"Frigus inspiratione,"* and Helesys echoed them aloud.

The tendril whip sprung forward, racing across the ground in a violent, lurching bolt. Frozen air pulsed from it—it looked as if the ground had been broken open, revealing a polar waste-land beneath. The brilliant white grew and grew until the tendril was upon the shaman and the light was blinding. It ended in a crash of thunder that shook the ground and the trees.

When Helesys opened her eyes, she saw the field was still and bare. The bugs were gone; the bones were scattered. The frost nearly was too; only a pattern remained, like the veins of a leaf. The ring… the ring was spent; the blue glow on her finger faded to mundane crystal and she no longer felt the painful tendril reaching through her hand…

Across the field, there was a dense ball of bramble, spiked brown and dark green thorns, which Riona had encased herself in. Only a scant bit of frost covered the branches.

"Metow mob carsis," the shaman called, her voice muffled by the thorns. Bramble erupted from the ground, racing away from Riona and toward Helesys. The ground split and tore as if a great tree had been uprooted.

Helesys narrowed her eyes and waited. Meanwhile, she called on her wand-arm and felt the energy churn within it, like a bottled storm. She waited until the bramble was close enough to touch. Helesys would give Riona hope of winning before she took it away.

"Siccum putredine."

A wall of mist erupted from Helesys like a dam ruptured and blew across the battlefield. The blight spell tore through the bramble, splintering the branches into shards and powder—sucking the life from them. Blight left ash and death in its wake.

Helesys followed. The weaver bolstered her strength and sprinted just behind the wave, unperturbed by the cloud of dead bramble, unperturbed by the psychic recoil of the spell—of the bubbling despair and bile taste in her mouth. She crossed the field in a half dozen strides.

Riona gasped as the wave decimated her bramble shield and then flailed in surprise as Helesys crashed through the powdered remains. "*Letabola!*" the shaman shouted.

The weaver tackled her, hoping to knock the wind from the shaman, but Helesys's shoulder slammed into something rough and dense. Helesys tackled her to the ground and knelt over her.

Riona's skin was covered in a wrinkled bark so dense it looked like plate mail. The bark around her face creaked and scraped as the plates around her mouth slid together into a smirk. The shaman grasped for Helesys's arms in attempt to fight her off. The barkskin spell bolstered Riona's strength—Helesys could feel as much from the shaman's struggle—but not to the levels of strength that Helesys could muster.

The men watched from the treeline, huddled and unmoving. Behind her, Helesys heard the rattle of broken bone creatures punctuated by shouts of rage.

"Call off the bonemen," Helesys growled.

"No."

Helesys wrenched her arms free, then punched the bark-covered shaman with her mundane hand, then her gauntlet.

Both strikes fell dully upon the bark. Riona laughed—a mix of a cackle and snapping branches.

Helesys called on her wand, siphoning more power. She had bolstered her arcane blasts, but never her strength in such a way. She felt as if she were reaching down into a well and dredging deep into untapped reserves. The hum of the gauntlet grew to a rattle, and the weaver felt power flow into her muscles, her bones. Her skin felt hot. Her hands shook.

This time when the weaver punched, bark splintered—another strike—shattered. The cackling stopped. Riona's arms flailed wildly now and yet they moved in slow-motion, easily brushed aside like sapling stalks.

Helesys broke the bark from her face, her shoulders. It came away bloody, taking slivers of cloth and skin from the shaman.

"Call them off!"

Riona's half broken face twisted in panic. "No!" She pawed desperately at her assailant. Helesys felt the slaps of wood against her arms, but they were distant, like a muffled echo.

The world grew quiet as the weaver set to task—old memories of violence returning. ...How easily they did.

Helesys grasped the bark around the shaman's neck and wrenched the remaining coverings free. She heard the muffled snaps of bark and even the faint tearing of skin, but they were no concern. She felt the weak impact of the shaman's fists against her arms, but they felt like a dream.

Helesys grabbed Riona's throat with her gauntlet, but didn't squeeze. She relaxed her strength just enough to concentrate on a second spell.

"*Progentibus Lucem.*" Her metal arm glowed with warding light. It was a potent spell, one used to repell fiends and ghastly creatures, with the side effect of turning the metal white-hot.

Riona's eyes grew wide despite the harsh light, and it cast horrid shadows across her face. The shaman thrashed, legs kicking, arms slapping. Discordant. Weak.

Helesys didn't stop until she smelled burning flesh.

"Call off the bonemen," Helesys said quietly. Her metal hand was hovering just off of the shaman, the light gone, the metal already cooling.

Riona stilled. Her hands gripped Helesys's arms, hanging onto her weakly.

"Call off the—"

"*Khutenri baba hark*," Riona whispered. Her eyes were closed, cheeks wet with tears.

Behind them, the battle was cut short.

~

And in the silent aftermath came footsteps of the men from the trees. They bore no weapons and went to the injured. Of the two men struck by her arcane blasts, only one was gasping. The other lay dead.

Helesys left the wounded shaman and walked to the gasping man. The guards that were tending to him backed away, hands raised.

Only one spoke. "Please don't hurt him."

Helesys wand-arm translated and she replied back in their tongue. "I intend to save him."

He lay crumpled on the ground. His right arm and right lay twisted, probably broken, but the bleeding wound on his side would claim him if left unattended. She knelt by his side and ripped the cloth tunic free. The skin was mangled, nearly gone from his ribs. Blood seeped down the muscle.

He looked at her, eyes half-open. Both scared and pleading.

"This will hurt, but it will stop the bleeding." Helesys said the words loud enough for the others to hear, for them not to interfere and break their tentative truce. She grasped his hand with her mundane one.

Again, she called on her warding light and her gauntlet grew white hot and blinding. She pressed the scalding metal to his side. The blood and skin sizzled, overshadowing his groan. He squeezed the weaver's hand. After several moments, Helesys released the power and the field grew dim again.

"It is done," Helesys said as she stood. She spoke to the guards without looking at them, for she didn't want to see their faces. "Tend to your wounded."

Taunauk was waiting for her, and she walked to him. The barbarian stood, chest heaving steadily, axe and shield still in hand. He was surrounded by piles of bones as if his ferocity had turned into a whirlwind, and swept up the whole bonefield. Still, two dozen more of the twisted bonemen wandered around. They picked at the scraps of the fallen and were planting them again in rows.

Helesys and Taunauk meant to walk away but were stopped short by a scream. They turned to see the guards backing away from a giant. It towered over the men, nearly thirty feet tall. It had the proportion of an ape, with long arms that hung nearly to the ground. It's body was gangly. It's splotchy, gray and purple skin was so thin that it showed the muscle and bone beneath despite the dark coloring. Its fingers were long and knobby like branches. It held one guard by the leg and dragged them away from the rest.

The men whispered, "Logath," as they hurriedly backed away.

In two great, shuddering steps, the giant stepped behind a tree—vanishing as if it were stepping through a doorway.

Meanwhile, the man screamed and pawed at the ground—screamed until he too disappeared behind the tree.

Taunauk said calmly, "Do you think it eats them?"

"No. Maybe…" It occurred to Helesys that Taunauk had not heard the words of the tribe. Her wand-arm translated for her ears alone. "I do not know. They spoke of the giant with reverence, as if it were a spirit of the forest." She shrugged. "Hopefully, that's enough to turn its attention away from us."

Taunauk grunted doubtfully.

When the giant was long gone and panic left the men, they helped up their wounded: The man Helesys had saved, and the shaman, whose throat Helesys had scorched.

Even from afar, Helesys could see the wound on her neck. It was a jagged red and in the shape of the weaver's metal hand—*gruesome*, Helesys thought. Yet of all her foes spared across the realms, Riona did not hurl back insults or curses in the aftermath. It was a fact not lost on her, yet one the weaver turned from in shame.

Helesys said, "Come, Taunauk. I am weary of this realm."

~

They crossed the bonefield, past the twisted denizens. The bonemen were free of the shaman's spell and paid no mind to the weaver and barbarian.

Though the pair watched the treeline and kept axe and gauntlet at the ready, they walked abreast and took solace in the moment. Words filled the quiet of the mist.

Taunauk said, "You did not have to save that man."

"I know." Helesys sighed. "I felt it necessary, though it does not undo the suffering caused. I maimed the shaman. She shall live with those scars."

"One cannot walk through the forest without breaking saplings underfoot. No, one good deed does not undo suffering, but it was good."

Helesys regarded her comrade. He walked tall, through an unknown forest as if he did not have a fear in the world—as if his cloak was not torn, his brow not smeared with dried sweat, his axe not coated in bone powder. He spoke the words without taking his eyes off the treeline. Still, they sounded as heartfelt as if he were looking her in the eye.

For a moment, her mind wandered back to the grievous wounds he suffered at the many hands of Shomosk in Zhug's cellar—when Helesys first used her warding light spell to cauterize a wound—but it was too painful a thought to remember him in such a state.

She said, "One day you will have to share where you learned all this wisdom."

The barbarian laughed a single heave. "One day, perhaps. When I can recall more than my name and a shadow of my past." A moment he added, "I do not envy you; yours was the harder fight. I struck against things that don't feel, don't suffer and don't question. It is an easy task, in comparison. Yours are truly the stronger shoulders, this day."

~ ~ ~

The Grotto of Irehyl

The weaver and the barbarian wandered the jungle, haunted by the squawks of birds and rustle of trees. They pressed forward, not knowing what they were looking for in this realm, only that they must press forward if they had any hope of escaping.

After some time, the ever-present fog broke and revealed a lush grotto. In the center was a crystal clear pond that shimmered with the reflection of faint fog from above. Beneath its glassy waters were orange and white koi fish. Flowers lined the waters' edge and glowed with radiant blues, greens, and golds, like stars brought to the earth. At the end of it all was a mound that rose up some two dozen feet high, covered with the same iridescent flowers.

Helesys's chest stilled and her mouth hung open at the sight. "Gods, what a site to be trapped here."

"Indeed. Strangely beautiful," Taunauk mumbled. Though his eyes were wide with wonder, he searched over the grotto.

It was only then, after Taunauk's words, that Helesys felt the faint kindling of her wand-arm—not so strong or foreboding as danger, but a mindful hint that they were in the presence of something magical and that the grotto was not mundane.

Before she could get a moment to whisper these things to Taunauk, the great mound began to shudder and then to move. Dirt broke free and rolled down to the base of it. Great coils emerged from the mass—a great, twisted, sleeping serpent woke. Its body was thicker than Taunauk's shoulders and covered in fine feathers—speckled white and grey, and smeared with mud from the grotto's edge. As the dirt fell away, it was clear that the flowers on its back were not just growing from the dirt, but protruding from the body of the beast.

Finally, the great head of the serpent emerged and it shot up into the air. It reached the height and bounds of the fog before turning sharply and plunging toward the grotto. It was only then that they saw the serpent had the face of a blue Terran woman—eyes closed peacefully, yet mouth open wide in a silent scream.

It—she—met the water in a graceful arc, then bounded across the surface of the water like a great stone skipping across it. Yet her feathered body seemed to float across the surface, never so much as making ripples.

After she bounded the length of the grotto, the serpent came to rest in the center of the pool. The full length of her coiled nearly end to end, some hundred feet long. Her body slackened as rested completely against the water's surface, and as it did, speckled feathers fell from her body and floated down to the bottom of the pool like lazy flakes of snow.

The head of the serpent was a dozen feet from Helesys and Taunauk, and she raised up enough so that the blue Terran face—nearly four feet from top to chin—was level with them.

Though Helesys arm still kindled with warmth, neither she nor Taunauk moved to ready their weapons.

"I am Irehyl. Goddess of the Indeppi. Goddess of the lost." She spoke the common tongue, or perhaps whatever tongue both the weaver and barbarian would understand. Her lips barely moved but her deep voice sounded over the water like a gong—Helesys sensed this was the gentlest voice the goddess could manage. All the while, her eyes were closed, as if she were sleeping.

"I am Helesys Byyra."

"I am Taunauk of clan Aonar."

"Why do you come to my grotto?" Irehyl asked.

Helesys said, "We wander the realms, seeking escape."

At this, the goddess smiled faintly. "Of the few souls I have seen, so few still seek escape. But then you are young in your wandering."

Taunauk said solemnly, "We would listen to wisdom, if you would share."

The goddess looked upon them with more than eyes and did this for a long moment before answering. "Taunauk and Helesys, I sense that you would listen, but I doubt that I have wisdom for any such as you."

"We seek the Wolf King and the Gatekeeper," Taunauk said, "but we are lost, goddess. We are in your grace."

The faintest flicker of emotion crossed the corner of her blue lips. "Those who forge their own path are not lost."

Helesys asked, "What do you know of those two? We have heard legends, and I have seen the Wolf King as he possessed another mage, but we know little of them."

"I know nothing more than the old legends: That the Wolf King sought her and bound himself to her."

Helesys hung her head, then asked, "Then have you any words for this realm? Any guidance? ...or might we perform a favor?"

Helesys did not know why she asked—it might have been an absurd question to ask of the goddess, but the great serpent rumbled in contemplation, sending ripples across the pond. Somewhere in the rumbling was Taunauk's own grunt of curiosity.

"Have you come across any tribes?" Irehyl asked.

The weaver and barbarian nodded. Helesys said, "We passed through the tribe that worships Logath. They are mad cannibals."

"Yes. Yes, they are," Irehyl said coldly. "Madness knows no race or creed. We are all susceptible to it. But it was not always so... Before the fog, the realm was lush as my grotto. Now, the tribes are isolated and blind to the world outside the shaman's lies. Perhaps... Perhaps there is something.

"At the edge of the forest lie the Damned. The magic that permeates this realm has desecrated them. They are beyond mad. Beyond lost. If you were to enter their nest, at the center will find a trapdoor and an underground passage. Follow it. At the heart of the underground you will find the Apothecary and the source of the sacred fire. Kill the Apothecary and end the fire."

Helesys glanced to her silent comrade, but his face was unreadable as stone. So she asked, "And that will lift the fog? What then?"

"Many things. Many more than happen now," the goddess replied.

"Why don't you do it?" Helesys asked. The question came out harsher than she meant it to. "It's just that... We've seen a great many incredible beings and yet they are all stagnant. They do nothing."

Now the blue face smiled warmly, eyes still closed. "For the same reason that the long lived do not wander as you do. We do not suffer one death here, but a thousand smaller ones. They erode us, hollow us, until we are a candle of our former selves. You are right to look upon your gods and question our silence and our absence, *but*... We are weary. Even Movernus, the prime, the immaterial, does not make anymore and had not for many years before I was trapped here.. Even he who feels all and made all, is weary. What hope does that give us small gods?"

Taunauk said quietly, "Time weathers all things, even here." The goddess nodded.

Helesys looked upon the goddess with a heavy heart. If even the gods ceased to hope, ceased to dream, ceased to act...

No, Helesys thought to herself. She would not dwell on it. Something kindled inside the weaver—a warmth not unlike the bolstering of her wand-arm, except that this came from herself. An inner strength not from magic and metal, but from her own breast.

"If one day we are ground to dust," Helesys said to Taunauk, "then so be it. If one day we sit quietly, trapped in a single realm, then so be it. But today is not *that* day. We will go forth—we who have few deaths behind us and many, many more ahead of us." She turned to the goddess. "We will kill the Apothecary and end the fog, and, at the least, the realm will be different for it."

For the first time, Helesys saw a flicker of movement behind the closed blue eyes. "Some will curse the change and others will praise it. Still more will hurl the same at the bringers of change. Should your many deaths bring you once again to our realm, then you will find new enemies and allies. Even if you are not lost, I shall count you as one of my steward's all the same."

The weaver nodded thankfully. Then said, "Surely, even your stewards and champions cannot be lost as those who seek you."

"They are as lost as my seekers, for no one calls the name Irehyl without having lost hope. And they are no more lost than I—for how could I offer guidance and wisdom were I not so? I could not feel their anguish, nor ease it, if I looked down on them from the stars."

They left and felt the goddess's closed eyes upon their back. *So many lost,* Helesys thought, *and so few goddesses to tend to them.*

~ ~ ~

The Nest of the Damned

Helesys and Taunauk pressed into the mist again. Toward the outer edge of the jungle, searching for the Nest of the Damned. And beyond that, the Apothecary—supposedly at the heart of it all.

Taunauk walked with axe in hand, half-ready for danger. "What if the serpent is wrong?"

Helesys glanced at her comrade but returned to keeping her eyes on the mist. "Is that an idle musing or a serious concern?"

Though she couldn't see him, she heard the scrunching of fabric and chainmail—the apathetic shrug of her comrade's massive shoulders. "I have no power to discern the truth," he added. "I felt the goddess was truthful."

"What reason would she have to lie?" Helesys asked.

"Gain, same as any mortal. What did your arm or your magic tell you?"

The weaver shrugged, mimicking her comrade, though neither of them saw the other. They were used to walking that way through the halls and through the forests of the realms—talking without looking at one another, lest some hidden danger seize the moment.

Helesys added, "Who do you trust more, a goddess or another weaver?"

Taunauk chuckled, "Forgive me. I remember few weavers: You, Amadeus, Matron Milde', and Zhug. Hardly enough to make a judgement."

"Don't forget the fishmen weavers. There were several of them."

"That hinders your case!"

Helesys chuckled, "You said once that you did not trust weavers. Are you having a change of heart?"

"That was when all I remembered of them was the fishmen weavers." The barbarian paused, the levity gone from his voice. "It may have been a false sentiment. Know that I do not count you among them."

Helesys smiled, and turned toward the outlander to thank him, but found him looking away, or maybe off into the mist. Maybe not content to bear his own emotions.

She said quietly, "Think nothing of it."

~

Time bled together in the blindness of the mist. They might've walked an hour through the jungle, or perhaps several—it was impossible to say. All the proceeding hours, Helesys had expected the fog to give way to the Nest of the Damned; expected that it would part, much as it did to reveal the beautiful grotto of Irehyl. No—it seemed that whatever forces presided here wished to hide the madness of the Damned.

But the Damned were not completely hidden, for the sounds of cackling laughter echoed in the distance. Somewhere in the fog.

Taunauk quietly drew Everfall. Helesys kindled her wand-arm, half bolstering her strength while the other half of her concentration fell upon the sheer power of her arcane blasts. Taunauk led them deeper into the mist and closer to the mad sounds.

Crumbling stone peaked up from out of the mist. The remnants of some ancient structure brought to its knees. Jagged, half-destroyed walls surrounded the pair; some sections no higher than a line on the ground. As they moved forward, an outline of stone walls grew more numerous, showing themselves in parallel lines to either side of them. Soon, Helesys was sure that they were walking through the remnants of a hallway.

Helesys thought of the crumbling gatehouse from the Wode and the civilizations ground beneath the inexorable passing of time. But this...this was no simple wear. In most sections, the ceiling was nearly gone. Some walls were broken and lay in splintered heaps as if they'd been broken with siege weapons or magic... The weaver glanced at her gauntlet, and imagined her own blasts tearing through the stone.

All the while, the mad laughter grew louder in the mist and from somewhere around the stones. A choir of discordant voices. Some shrill, some hoarse, others water-logged as if they were drowning on land.

Taunauk stopped suddenly, and Helesys heard the squeezing of his hand on the battleaxe. She leaned close to the stone and peered around him in the narrow hallway.

In front of them, blocking their path, was a crouched Terran figure at the edge of the mist. Even half-shrouded, Helesys could see the thin, knobby frame. As it crawled forward, its full horrid appearance came into view. At first, it resembled the half-made creatures from the boneyard. But this creature was covered in thin, red muscle. There were few patches of skin:

One on its cheek, torso and right arm. The edges of the skin and the whole of the muscles were weeping blood. Patches of wiry hair stuck to its skull in the few places flesh was left. It's eyes were sunken and lidless, yet had bright green dots amidst the black. It stared at Helesys and Taunauk with a gory, curious look.

It opened its mouth and bared its yellow, crooked teeth and let out a throaty cackle. Then it sprang forward, gnarled hands outstretched.

In one swift motion, Taunauk's axe cleaved through the creature from shoulder to hip. The creature continued laughing and reaching feebly, even as it crumpled against the stone wall.

The cackling grew,as if the mist was bubbling with laughter. Then there was a scratching and scurrying of grotesque limbs over the stone—from all around them.

Helesys turned to see two twisted creatures skittering toward her, practically clawing their way over one another to get to her. She raised her gauntlet and let go an arcane blast—a silent answer to their madness. The blast tore through the pair, severing limbs and quieting them as they were blown back into the mist.

Helesys felt hands reaching for her hair—from over the stone, but she grasped them, pulled them down, then pummeled them with magic-enhanced strength. Their skulls shattering like over ripened fruit—even as her eyes went wide in shock, Helesys did not slow or stutter.

Instantly, the decrepit stone hallway became a frenzy. Helesys was a whirl, lashing out with her limbs, elbows, knees, and blasting with her gauntlet to fend off those that dared come at her directly from the hall. Meanwhile, the stone walls shuddered as Taunauk lashed out with Everfall, crunching enemies against the stone and splitting others two at a time with his battleaxe.

Still, they came. In spite of the bodies and the carnage piling up at their feet. The violence and the cackling grew.

Taunauk shouted, "Follow me!"

The barbarian leveled his shield and barreled down the hallway like a battering ram. Helesys turned and followed at his heels, a mundane palm pressed against his back. Only half-looking, she sprayed arcane blasts behind her as they ran. She couldn't tell how many creatures she hit, only that their laughter stuttered with each successive casualty. Others flew overhead as Taunauk ran through them or bounced limply off the walls as the barbarian broke through their wild ranks. Others leapt from overtop the broken walls and rolled off the barbarian's shoulders like rain.

They passed clear breaks and Helesys could see the mist swirling wildly beyond, filled with their crazed pursuers. They followed the turns of the stone hallway—left, right, left, left—until Helesys could no longer discern what direction they were heading and all she knew was the frenzy of the run.

The stone hallway gave way completely, and they came to a clearing. Here, the mist broke slightly so that they could see some fifty feet across. At the center, rose a giant stone statue. At first, it appeared to be a centaur, but it had clawed feet and the texture of scales across the whole of it—a serpent who had grown six legs and merely stood in the posture of a centaur.

Beyond the clearing was another massive pillar inlaid with familiar geometric carvings. Just past it was a stone archway and the remnants of a domed building. Most of it had fallen away and lay crumpled around the edges. Through the archway, Helesys could see the edge of a trapdoor on the ground.

Helesys and Taunauk whirled around and stood back to back, ready for battle. The cackling surrounded them, coming from all around the clearing, but none of the Damned approached or even came close enough that they could be seen through the mist.

The weaver asked quietly, "Do you see the trapdoor across the way?"

Taunauk grunted in affirmation. "Stay close."

The pair stalked forward, circling each other so as to watch all angles—a slow dance of readied death. Axe and metal arm waiting for any foolish enough to cut in.

As Helesys was facing the mist, Taunauk growled. The weaver turned and felt the ground shudder beneath her feet. From the statue came a great towering thing, a giant made of sinew and red flesh as tall as the stone statue. It reached a massive hand toward them—but rather than a single being, it was made of the hundreds of the Damned. The hand was not a single thing; each finger was one of the creatures and reached toward them with a silent scream and outstretched arms.

Helesys's stomach turned in disgust and she leveled her wand-arm—not content to wait until it was closer. Arcane energy blasted the twisted hand. The fingers were broken off, remnants hung limply from where the knuckles might have been. Only when she blasted the palm of the beast did the creature recoil—revealing splotchy, gray and purple beneath the outer layer.

"Logath," Helesys mumbled. "It wears their bodies."

The flesh-covered giant stepped back behind the statue and vanished without a sound. Not even a footstep.

The weaver and outlander returned to their battle ready stance with anticipation.. The Damned did not disappoint.

Twisted men descended upon them like rushing flood waters, their cackles echoing over each other like bubbling waves. Teeth bared in madness and violence.

The weaver and barbarian met them with even greater ferocity. Helesys drained her bolstered strength and siphoned nearly all of it to raw power. She braced herself and let loose spreadblasts from her gauntlet that tore across the battlefield like a tidal water, each nearly as wide as her field of vision, each digging craters of earth in their path and blowing away dozens of the Damned at a time—silencing whole sections of the battlefield.

Still more came. The mad creatures clambered over the fallen. No amount of death dissuading them.

Out of the corner of her vision, she saw Taunauk glowing, golden flames flickering off him. She had no trouble picturing the power-laden barbarian slicing through an equal amount with each massive arc of his battleaxe.

Even as the blasts rattled her shoulder and pushed her heels into the dirt, she kept firing. The carnage blurred around her and the world grew quiet—distractions faded away. Again, she felt as if she were trusting her body and her wand-arm. trusting training and memories of battle—feeling as if her body were fighting *for her.*

The massive hand of Logath returned, covered with fresh Damned, reaching down toward her, and the suddenness of it broke her entrancement. Helesys turned her gauntlet toward the giant and fired. The weaver gritted her teeth against the recoil and the blast washed across Logath's arm, tearing the lesser bodies from it.

The giant roared in anguish and clutched its bare and blood-ied arm. For the first time, Helesys looked upon the face and body of the giant, covered with writhing, silent bodies.

In that moment, the assault stopped—as if the creatures were halted by the giant's pain.

"Run for the door," Helesys said.

The weaver and the barbarian sprinted across the clearing, golden flames fading from his arms and cloak. Helesys bol-stered her speed, and they crossed the clearing on superhuman strides.

As they neared the carved pillar. Logath's covered hand reached out from behind it, descending toward the pair with eerie speed. Instead of shooting the writhing hand, Helesys aimed for the pillar, churned power and blasted it. The purple fireball seared the giant's hand and then plowed through the column, shattering through it. The giant twisted away in sur-prise, vanishing behind the column and from sight as quickly as it had appeared.

Then the jungle groaned. A low rumble echoed through the fog, seemingly from all around, and even from above. Then came deep snaps, like the breaking of old wood. The loudest were from the column in front of them—the one that Helesys had broken. Even though she had blasted clean through it, the top portion hung in the air for a moment, as if it wasn't a single column, but merely a part of something greater whose struc-ture lay in the sky high above the mist. But then it too came crashing down like a great pike driven into the ground. Then cracks echoed up the length of it, and Helesys knew the calam-ity was not over—that the rest of the great structure would fall to the ground along.

Helesys and Taunauk had paused for only a moment, but she feared even that was too much. The sky shook so fierce and loud that it sounded as if it was falling on top of them. They sprinted across the rest of the field, through the archway and into the broken dome, to where the massive trapdoor waited for them.

Taunauk stowed his axe and shield, bent down and grasped under the trapdoor. Then he roared and pulled, the great bulk of the door groaning deeply, yet still overshadowed by the roar of the sky and shattering column. The ground shook with each massive impact as sections of the column fell to the ground.

Helesys turned and saw the swirling mass of mist and the Damned emerging a moment later. She met them with arcane death and wave after wave of power shattered their ranks. But still they clambered over the dead and the broken, stepping over the fallen in a mad dash toward the weaver and barbarian. The sound of the shattering of the sky above them was drowned out by violence.

And just before Taunauk yelled for his comrade, just before they escaped, Helesys saw a stirring of the mist above them. Pieces of sky were falling—or so she thought at first. Great sections some miles across shown through the mist as they fell toward the ground. She ducked under the trapdoor and saw the faint starlight and deep blue black sky through the cracks. Whatever structure had blotted out the sky was falling.

Helesys slipped under the door, and the barbarian followed. The pair slid down the steep slope, down slick rock and sheer drops, down a jagged borehole some ten feet across. Helesys flared the light of her wand-arm as the pair slipped deeper and deeper, desperate to get away from the falling sky above them.

Before they reached the bottom, the world shook violently, as if the very ground under, above, and around them might come apart at the seams. Helesys and Taunauk paused on an outcropping of rock, chests heaving. Caught between the violence above and the unknown below.

~ ~ ~

The Cellar

In the deafening silence that followed, dust fell from above—and thankfully, nothing more. The light from her gauntlet shone brightly and made the floating dust look eerily like the mist.

"Are you alright?" Taunauk asked.

"Yes," Helesys replied quickly. She did not want to speak further, not while the dust was falling.

Above them, the trapdoor loomed. Still and shut. They waited, but no sound came from above. After a minute, Helesys waved for the barbarian to follow and she led them down the sloped passageway, keeping her light at her hip.

The air grew cool, and they heard the faint drips of water somewhere in the cavern. The borehole turned into a passageway that curved around on itself, like a spiral staircase, for some thousand feet before leveling off. Jagged rock gave way to wooden planks. Those planks beneath their feet were worn smooth and occasional planks on the walls and ceiling were missing entirely.

"A mine," Helesys whispered. "What purpose would a mine have in a place such as this?"

Taunauk shrugged. "Do you remember the queen of the hive? Perhaps they dug to escape, just as she did."

She remembered; the queen was as trapped as its pitiful slaves. "It is folly," she finally said.

"Our follies that raise men from beasts."

Helesys said, "Curious that you think it's our follies and not our hopes or dreams. Or that Terrans should be above beasts at all."

Taunauk replied plainly, "The wild dog salivates during the hunt, hoping for success. But a lost hunt is only an empty belly, perhaps a resolve to hunt differently or faster. Terrans feel shame in their follies—in that, we are different."

Helesys smiled faintly, for she could not disagree with his logic. Despite her comrade's insights, they still seemed a peculiar event—perhaps it was that Taunauk mused without weapons in hand—with a mind as keen as steel. Regardless, she felt compelled to follow the thought.

"Are all outlanders as philosophical as you?"

"How presumptuous of you… to think that I remember other outlanders." The barbarian's face softened at the joke. "Come." He drew his axe and led them deeper into the mine.

~

The silence drug on, save for their bootsteps on the planks. They followed the passageway for a half dozen twists and turns before coming to a doorway and a small, empty room lined with metal beams and wood planks.

"A dead end," Taunauk said.

But Helesys recognized the contraption. "No. It is like the dumbwaiter. See the rails?"

She pointed along the edges, to a track that descended into the mines. The weaver searched with her wand and found the remnants of magic in the contraption. As far as she could tell, the lingering magic didn't feel malicious or defensive.

Helesys cautiously stepped forward, keeping her senses focused on the latent magic of the contraption. She bolstered her strength, in case some hidden ward lashed out at her, but none came. The elf stepped all the way into the elevator and breathed a sigh of relief.

"Seems safe enough," she said. "These rails will take us down into the mines, and, if Irehyl is truthful, to the Apothecary."

Taunauk stalked forward, eyes darting to the corners of the enclosure. Slowly, he stepped entirely inside, and the room felt all the smaller for his bulk.

On the wall beside the door was a set of four levers. Helesys tried the first, but save for the clink of the metal lever, nothing happened. The same anticlimax happened for all four. She tried several levers at a time, but no two levers elicited a response.

Frustrated, she turned her gauntlet toward the contraption and tried to sense the hidden connection. "There must be a combination or *something...*"

Helesys trailed off because an image flashed in her mind: The stone statue of the centaur-like reptile from above. It stood on four legs and had four more arms. She looked upon the levers anew, but they were spaced in such a way that she could not pull all at the same time.

"Taunauk, we must flip all four levers at the same time."

The barbarian set his axe against the corner and grasped two of the levers. When all four were flipped, two doors slid closed, and the car slid downward with a soft squeak of metal.

Both sighed and Taunauk picked his axe back up.

"What did you see?" he asked.

"I saw the statue from above," Helesys replied, still half-entranced by the image and how her wand-arm showed it to her. "This place must have been built by the serpent creatures… and I feel they are long gone. Like the clam-faced creatures that predated the fishmen. Gods, there have been so many trapped here."

The barbarian nodded in solemn agreement.

In the quiet hum of the descending room, Helesys wanted to fill the silence. There were so few times in their journey across the realms that they had quiet moments, that they were not sneaking past danger or sleeping in shifts. So little time they had for conversation and so little they remembered to converse about.

She asked, "Have you thought any more on your golden glow?"

Taunauk bowed his head and stared at the wall, or perhaps through it. "I still do not understand it."

In their journeys, the barbarian had explained to her the secret of Endroggen rage—the ferocity, strength, and superhuman fortitude that the barbarians have in battle. He confessed to her that it was blood magic; a deep and personal magic passed down through the generations of family line.

"Twice now, you said, *we*, when replying with your glow. At first I thought you were speaking of you and I… Are you sure there is no other voice but your own?"

"I… I cannot say."

Unperturbed, Helesys asked, "Is it similar to your blood magic?"

"No. If the powers are both wells from which to draw strength, then rage is a well from within myself, of my own making. The glow is far deeper and far more potent… It is not mine. It is from *somewhere else.*" Though Taunauk spoke with certainty, the admission seemed difficult for him.

"I remember an outlander who did not wish to owe their power to any other." She said the words with an air of levity, and in the moment she felt as if she were channeling Shawn. He would've appreciated the lighthearted jab.

Taunauk smirked—a quick a fleeting emotion—the first time she had seen such a reaction from the unpresuming outlander. "The power is not from within me, but it is familiar. It echoes, the same as my axe did. The power *is mine*, as if by birthright." Taunauk shook his head. "But I still do not understand it."

The descending room squealed to a halt, ending their conversation, and the twin doors slid open.

~

Taunauk went first into the hallway with axe in hand, with Helesys and her light at his back. In front of them, a narrow hallway extended into darkness. The whole of it was lined with crooked, musty planks of wood, which creaked beneath their feet.

An unnerving chill fell over Helesys as they pressed into the hall, punctuated by a hum of warning from her wand-arm—something she recognized all too well.

"We are getting close to the Apothecary," she said. "These halls are warded with magic."

As if on cue, the planks of the hall began to rattle, shaking on whatever feeble nails held them in place. The shaking rolled toward them, like a wave beneath the floor, buckling the wood. It rolled under their feet, lifting both the weaver and barbarian up into the air, before passing under them and ending at the descending room.

Then came the cackle of the Damned.

Taunauk growled and stalked forward. Helesys followed, lowering the light and shunting power to bolster her strength and to the blast of her gauntlet. Both of them stared down the hall with steely determination, ready to shake off whatever attack might come.

Something grabbed Helesys's mundane left arm. Instinctually, she braced herself and turned to see a twisted, flayed arm of the mad creatures had reached through the planks of the wall. Fingertips of others were reaching through the planks.

Helesys turned her metal arm toward the wall, toned down the blast, and fired. The purple power shattered the arm, and it slunk back through the boards with a whimper. Three more arms clambered and sprung from the gap.

Behind her, she heard the slices of Taunauk's axe, and she turned to see four rended arms laying bloody on the floor.

The cackles of the Damned and the wooden groans of planks grew loud, and again the wood of the hall rattle. The hallway came alive as hundreds of hands reached for the intruders.

"Forward!" Helesys shouted. She burned her wand-arm, and fired around Taunauk and down the hall. The arcane energy sailed through dozens of the creatures, burning dozens and breaking more, as the purple ball ricocheted off the planks.

Taunauk charged, swinging his axe at the Damned that hadn't been dissuaded by the blast. He swung without missing a stride, and Helesys timed three more blasts around her comrade as they ran. They plowed through the hallway in their own destructive wave, and the creatures wilted before them.

As they passed, Helesys blasted those few arms that survived their onslaught and still reached out to her. One of these close and particularly violent blasts ripped the planks from the wall of the tunnel—Helesys feared that she had opened a doorway and that the creatures would pour through and give chase—but there was only dirt beneath. The Damned were reaching through from somewhere else with the help of the Apothecary's magic.

In front of them, a massive hand emerged from the floorboards, knobby, gray and purple—the hand of Logath. It's massive fingers blocked their path and then the full length of the arm reached through the boards and snaked toward them.

Taunauk met it with a flurry of axeswings, but instead of cutting through, the blade slid harmlessly over the creature's skin. The barbarian roared in frustration, pulled Everfall from his back and used the ironwood shield to bat and bash away the approaching hand. Impacts shook the cavern and each gave the giant pause.

Helesys backed away, leveled her gauntlet toward the beast, and channeled both her arcane blast and the power of her crystal ring. The power of frost swirled with arcane death, and she unleashed a blast that nearly knocked her over. The recoil shook her shoulder and the blast pummeled the giant's arm.

In the space between, Logath cried out in surprise and the arm retracted, snaking back through the impossible gap in the floorboards, back into some magical space between realms.

Helesys and Taunauk ran past the broken boards and past the ever-grasping hands of the creatures, down the hallway toward whatever dangers and wards lay in wait.

~

They ran past the gnarled hands of the Damned, cutting them down in stride, and finally came to an empty section of passageway. Here, the hands ended abruptly and vanished completely once Helesys and Taunauk crossed some unseen threshold.

They stopped and waited for a trap, but none came. Nor did they see Logath's hand.

"Do you sense anything?" Taunauk asked, facing down the empty corridor with steely determination.

Helesys focused on her wand-arm, opening her senses to any nearby magic… and it was unlike anything she had ever felt: Magic loomed all around and permeated the earth surrounding them, yet it was not the same magic as the guards and wards she had felt in the sanctum of Amadeus, the wizard that told them the terrible secret of the dungeon.

Here in the mines, it was as if she could feel the very magic that held the dungeon together, as if it were bubbling up out of every grain of dirt and every floorboard.

"I sense magic," she said tentatively, "but I don't believe they are wards or traps. The weave, the magic embodiment of the world, feels weak here." She ran a hand over the rough wall. "Almost as if I could reach out and grasp it."

Touching the boards did nothing, but added to Helesys's wonder all the same.

"To task," the barbarian said. Taunauk led them down the mine.

The passageway stretched on, before ending abruptly and modestly at a wooden door.

Before Helesys and Taunauk could discuss or prepare, a ragged woman's voice came from beyond. "Come in, dearies."

~ ~ ~

The Apothecary

The humble door opened to a sprawling underground room, much wider than it was tall. Both Taunauk and Helesys stooped to avoid hitting their heads on the threshold and stepped through with readied weapons.

The room inside was cut from the surrounding earth—there were no wooden boards to soften the illusion or even dust to soften the lines. Here was hard stone, a fitting counter to the mist that plagued the surface of the realm. Barrels and casks lined the wall. A cluttered table sat in the corner, littered with bottles and vials, their contents bubbling or opaque, forming a haphazard rainbow. Meat hooks hung from the wall in equal fashion, some spaced so close together they looked unusable; small animal skins were splayed and hung across multiple hooks—both the weaver and barbarian would be remiss if they were to walk carelessly. The floor was completely bare, jagged rock.

There was a single passageway beyond the table and it extended out into darkness and from the darkness walked a woman. She wore a harsh black robe, one that looked burnt and charred, but belied her slender form and fitting height for such a room. The next, immediate thing that Helesys noticed was that the woman was beautiful, her face slender and soft, hair so black that it disappeared beyond the hood of her robe. Her steps were graceful across the stone, and her hands were hidden within her long sleeves.

"My, my, it's been such a long time since someone has wandered so far—and two someones, no less!" Her hoarse voice was a stark contrast to the beauty she extolled. She pointed an accusing finger toward Taunauk and then Helesys. "An animal wearing the skin of another and a knife-eared experiment gone wrong."

"Charming," Taunauk growled.

Helesys wondered briefly whether he was more offended at the slur hurled at him or at her. "Are you always so charming to your guests?"

The woman cackled, and for a moment, her teeth flashed from white to yellow and back again. "Only those that plan to kill me. Though most that make it this far have violent agendas. Tell me, am I wrong?" Neither Helesys nor Taunauk answered, and so she continued. "What foul wanderers stand before the Apothecary?"

"Taunauk Aonar."

"Helesys Byyra."

"And how long will you cling to the old names, *mithral-skin?*"

Helesys eyes narrowed. "Do you even remember yours?"

"The old name is the first part that dies."

Helesys replied, "Then you are just as pitiful as the others. Tell me, *witch*, are you the cause of the cannibal's bonfire and the cause of the mist that plagues the realm?"

The Apothecary glared at her, left iris flickering from green to red and back. "I am all that you suspect."

"Then defend your—" Helesys's threat was cut short by the hand of Logath. The giant's hand burst through the wall, some arcane seam in the rock, and seized Helesys. She tried to turn and raise her gauntlet to meet it, but Its hand enveloped her from shoulder to knee, pinning her arms across her stomach. As its hand clamped down, Helesys flared her wand-arm, bolstering her muscles and her bones to keep from being crushed.

The last things she saw were Taunauk's anger, eyes wide and teeth bared, and the slash of his axe—too slow to save her—

And the solemn grin of the Apothecary. "No mercy. No quarter."

Helesys lurched and felt her boots knock against the stone as Logath pulled her through the wall, leaving Taunauk to face the witch alone.

~

The world was awash with blurred greens and blues, of mist and confusion—some twisted mirror of the jungle above. The giant still held her in his hand, but where her face was free, the feeling of cold underground air on her cheeks was gone, and replaced with... stillness. There was no sensation of warmth or cold, or even wind.

Logath brought her to his face. As she looked upon the giant, Helesys realized that its appearance was also warped. Its splotchy skin smudged to a light purple. Its body and legs disappeared somewhere below in a blur, as if the giant were standing in a pool of water. Its glowing eyes were muted and unsavory. It glared at her with recognition.

She assumed the giant wasn't squeezing her, and so for the moment, her bolstered strength was managing.

Helesys said quickly, "Do you speak?"

Logath nodded, eyes locked on her.

"Then please, let me go."

The giant shook his head, *no*.

"So be it."

Helesys kept her strength and channeled the rest of the wand's power to her warding light. White light seeped out from between Logath's bony fingers. Her gauntlet grew scalding hot. Helesys felt the warmth, smelled the burning of her cloak, then finally felt pain as the gauntlet ebbed beyond her bolstered tolerance.

Logath's eyes slowly widened, as if the surprise of such a feat took time to register. Then it bellowed and recoiled in pain, and finally let go of her.

And Helesys's stomach turned as if she were falling, though she didn't move. She stayed facing Logath, hovering with nothing beneath her feet. The giant turned back to her. Helesys kindled her wand-arm and contemplated her options.

She said, "*Dissolvere vincula*," trying to break the apothecary's hold over the giant, but the magic powers of the witch ran deep. They felt like dozens of needles shoved into the giant's skin, far too many and far too deep for Helesys to absolve.

Logath swatted at her like she was a gnat, but Helesys slipped beyond its reach—moving without moving in the realm between realms. Again, a look of surprise came over its face, as if Logath were not used to its prey evading it so easily in its own realm.

Instead of countering, Helesys said, "*Restu sonmuvo, giganto.*" This time, the giant's body seemed to crystallize into view as if it were standing before her and it moved in a stuttering motion.

Helesys felt Logath's mind—primitive and child-like. The giant was quick to emotion, but its—his—impulses had been tempered by the witch's magic. Helesys felt the jabs of every needle-point, the burn of every tonic forced down the giant's throat. She tasted the salty scraps of the Terran meat and Helesys gagged—Terrans that Logath had dragged away for the Apothecary's research.

And as Helesys stomach turned again, she felt her hold on Logath dissolving. The very needles of magic that kept hold of the giant kept others from affecting him.

The weaver felt a pang of sadness for the giant, for his forced servitude to the witch and for the last of his emotions that he felt: Logath would not let Helesys go back willingly and he would not let Helesys harm the witch.

Necessary grief—fleeting grief—for what she had to do.

Helesys let go of the spell, then said, "*Lente et gravis.*"

Though Logath swatted at her again, his massive hands slowed to a crawl, as if he were dropped in sludge. Helesys blasted both hands, before floating toward the giant's chest. Logath had just begun to recoil when she reached him.

She funneled power to the raw blasts of her gauntlet, then bolstered them with the power of the crystal ring. Then Helesys pressed her metal hand to his bony chest and released a powerful blast—meant for gods and monsters—on the giant. She felt the piercing wound smolder and dissolve, then break and scatter of bone and flesh with wet, hollow sounds. She felt the recoil jolt through her shoulder and push her away.

Helesys floated backwards into the swirling greens and blues of the world between. The last she saw of Logath was the look of muted surprise on his face, before he blurred to a mix of reddish purple.

The weaver turned toward the swirling emptiness and con-
centrated, calling on the hidden well of knowledge in her wand.
Numerous times, she had remembered spells and counterspells as moments called for them—as if her mind needed
prompting to overcome the amnesia of the dungeon. Helesys
thought of countering the Apothecary's magic that made the
rift… Some kind of magic that let the witch tear open a hole
in the realm. The elf held out her metal hand—

—She felt it! She felt the rift that Logath used. Something
akin to a seam in fabric, yet bubbling and rippling as if it were
alive.

"*Amplificare potentia!*"

Instead of countering the witch's magic, Helesys bolstered
it. Amplified it. Her gauntlet shook with exertion.

The rippling grew to a pulse, the bubble to a boil.

Helesys flared her power and tore open the seam.

~

The Apothecary's dwelling came into view again. The witch
was backing toward the single hallway that led deeper into her
dwelling. Her beautiful dark hair was wild and hung in sweaty
strands over her face. Her robe was torn, and she clutched it
in one hand and hurled a yellow-green vial through the air with
the other.

Taunauk was in the center of the room, his skin and vest
glowing. His robe lay behind him on the rocky floor, charred
and burnt. Orange flames of power flickered off his shoulders.
The light was so powerful that even the axe in his hands and
shield upon his back seemed to glow.

The glass vial hit Taunauk in the chest and shattered. The
smoky liquid quickly faded against the barbarian's well of

power. Two more vials flew across the room and broke pitifully on him.

"Impossible!" The Apothecary hissed, "Those poisons are enough to kill one hundred men!"

Helesys stepped through the tear in the realm, through the rocky wall of the witch's dwelling, and felt gravity return as her feet touched the stone. Her stomach turned with the sensation.

The witch turned, her astonishment turning to anger as she looked upon Helesys. "*You*! What magic have you given him?"

"Nothing of your concern," Helesys replied, gauntlet raised and churning with power. She stepped forward and stood to the side of her comrade who glowed like a molten statue.

The Apothecary stepped behind the table adorned with vials. "You leave me no choice." She grasped the table and flipped it with demonic strength, sending the table and its contents flying across the room. Helesys fired a spreadblast as wide as she could. The vials shattered in a wash of light and darkness, acrid smoke and sweet-smelling poison, of lust and decay—for a moment Helesys was blinded. Her sight came back just in time to see her glowing companion slice through the table and send its halves crashing to the sides of them.

Cackling, the witch smiled and shattered an empty vial on the ground. "You have taken a servant from me. Now I shall have two more to replace him."

Helesys fired at her, but the purple blast phased through the witch, her form swirling as if she was made of smoke. Her mad laughter rose, and the witch began to grow, Her shoulders brushed against the ceiling, so tall that she was forced into a crouch. Yet, as she grew, her form became translucent.

Her voice deepened, "No matter how much strength you channel or what magics you wield, no one can sustain *the twisting*. I shall slip inside your pores like a thousand needles, wrench my grasp upon your bones and make you my puppet. Your mind will not be your own. Your eyes, your ears, your tongue will be mine." The witch was billowing now, her head and shoulders stretching across the ceiling like a trapped storm cloud and her legs were flowing across the floor, creeping their way toward Helesys and Taunauk. "I will quench your voice, extinguish hope. Fear and doubt will grow in their place and you will lose yourself in the jungle of your own prison."

While the witch boasted, Helesys's wand-arm hummed with warning, and Helesys's mind turned with how to counter this new magic. Both Helesys and Taunauk stepped back from the approaching smoke—the first time she had seen the barbarian do so in his golden form.

As Helesys regained her faculties and her memories in the dungeon, she was beginning to think of magical combat as a battle of wits, rather than one of strength or even skill. A surprise—especially one quick and decisive—was what she needed. The witch would count on her to cower and defend herself with bolstered strength and arcane blasts. Clearly the blasts would not work, and the strength of a giant could not overcome the Apothecary.

Helesys thought of the magic of the seams and tears, the rippling and bubbling. Of water brought to a boil and turning to steam. She smirked and stopped concentrating on her bolstered strength, clenched her teeth at the quiet pain of her injuries, and instead prepared to flare her power in one catastrophic push.

The Apothecary bellowed, "*You dare smile at me, weaver?*"

"I do. *Amplificare potentia!*"

And with the words, Helesys focused on the magic that was making the Apothecary grow large and turn to smoke. She dug deep in her well of power, trawling the depths. Then she amplified the witch's magic. Just as she had torn open the seam between realities, Helesys grasped the bubbling essence of the witch and amplified the spell.

The Apothecary's bellow turned to a roar as every puff and swirl of her was wrenched apart and scattered like dust in the wind.

Silence fell over the room, but still Taunauk glowed and held fast his axe. Helesys sensed from her wand-arm that the amplification spell was lost—she could no longer feel the witch's presence. Helesys relaxed her arm and slowly her comrade did the same.

The flames smoldered and left him. "You are as cunning as you are powerful." He looked up for a moment, as if he were wistfully following the flames' departure.

Helesys pressed forward. "And you are as indestructible. Come. Let us find the flame that the serpent spoke of and put an end to this."

She kindled her warding light and led the way down the dark passageway. She walked slowly, methodically, keeping a careful focus on her wand-arm, lest the witch have any last surprises for intruders. But as they followed the snaking passageway, there were no more traps to be had and soon Helesys's light was overshadowed by roaring flames.

They came to an open cavern and a roaring, incomprehensible fire. The curve of the cavern's walls suggested it arced around some hundred or even hundreds of feet, and rose to the same towering height above them, but they could not see the full size of it for the fire blotted out the room. The fire sprawled out so wide that it touched the walls and so high that it reached up to the cavern ceiling. It encompassed so much of the room that there was only a small section by the passageway entrance where they could stand. Bones and carved totems adorned this space—relics and foci for the late Apothecary's dark magic.

A fire of this magnitude should've been unbearable at a distance, yet the heat of the fire was muted, so much that they could stand in the room and within several feet of it. Only when Helesys reached a hand to within several inches of it did she feel the true heat of the fire.

Taunauk finally stowed his axe and reached a hand toward the magic inferno, recoiling at the same distance as the weaver did. "How are we to end the flames?"

Helesys reached out with her gauntlet again. She tried to sense any origins, any patterns, any hint to the making and sustaining of the flames—anything that might lead to their *unmaking*. The magic of the Apothecary was powerful, of that Helesys had no doubt. The magic of potions and elixirs was much different than the weaver was familiar—truly an art all its own. This great fire was equally different, and also deeply embedded in the cavern. It was not unlike the wards or spellguards that the wizard, Amadeus, had infused into his sanctum. The magic of the fire had smoldered long, like a deep stain in the ground.

Yet no matter the magic, there was always a source: A kernel, log or seed—a single spell. *Something* lay at the heart of the flame. Something powerful.

But Helesys had to reach the center and disrupt the source if she were to stop the bonfire. Counterspells could not quench the fire from the outside—not with such powerful, embedded magic.

Helesys searched her abilities, then settled on using the crystal ring. Its powers of frost and winter had staved off the fire of Amadeus's dragon.

She focused on the crystal ring and called forth the whip-like tendril of frost. She grit her teeth at the sensation of the cold snaking its way along her arm, along her bones—a most unpleasant sensation, but a necessary one. The white tendril of power coiled in the air around her, poising like a serpent and waiting for her command. With her gauntlet, Helesys amplified her strength and fortitude to their limits in preparation.

At her beckon, the tendril plunged into the fire. Even with the strength of a barbarian, Helesys felt the singeing of heat along her nerves, and the pain grew as the tendril pushed deeper into the heart of the fire. Her muscles shook with the pain and the quivering of her legs brought Helesys to her knees. The pain became a weight upon her shoulders, doubling her over. She pressed her gauntlet to the ground while her mundane hand and the crystal ring were raised to the fire.

And when she was nearly to the center, when the pain became unbearable, she saw the golden glow of Taunauk's boots. Then Helesys felt a hand upon her shoulder and with it came warmth.

Instead of pain, she felt light, as if the weight were being lifted from her shoulders. And with it came memory: Helesys was drawn back to some deep seated childhood time—to a memory so old and so lost beneath both her own psyche and the oppression of the dungeon, that it was no more than *a feeling* of memory. Helesys felt like a child again, like she was taking her first steps. From over her shoulder came the reassuring voices of her mother and her father as Helesys strode forth on wavering legs. The sensation was as blurry as looking through a pond's surface in a rainstorm, painted with broad, abstract strokes, yet it was as real and as powerful to her as if she could turn back and see their faces.

In the moment, the pain and anguish of the fire did not feel so heavy—for Helesys felt like she had the strength of ten barbarians.

Helesys rose to her feet, the glowing hand still upon her shoulder, and she willed the whip of frost to plunge to the center of the fire, stretching to its absolute limits. She felt something in the center of the fire, and with a scream of effort and anguish, she wrapped the tendril around it and heaved it toward her, wrenching herself backward and off her feet. She fell to the ground. The tendril of frost came with her, pulling a large bone out of the fire.

The fire roared. Sounds of cracking and tearing sounded from inside it, and the flames flickered from orange to green and finally to a shimmering aurora of colors. Then it vanished—its sudden disappearance leaving a void in the room that seemed to suck the very air with it.

~

A few moments later, Helesys caught her breath and turned to the bone on the ground beside her. It was circular, dense, and nearly a foot long. Helesys rose to a knee and looked from the bone to the top of the cavern, now shrouded in darkness.

Taunauk knelt down beside her, regarding her and the bone. "That was quite the feat."

Helesys nodded. "On both our parts. How… How did you channel the power?"

The barbarian shook his head. "I am not sure, but the more I wield it, the more in tune with it I become. What of that?"

He gestured toward the bone. "It is from the back of a creature. An immense one."

The weaver shook her head. "I do not know what is right to do with it."

She stood, examined the cavern and felt small in the new-found space. There were no passages, save for the one they came through... There were no paths forward.

Taunauk followed her gaze. "We shall retrace our steps. We can explore the rest of the realm."

Helesys sighed in dissatisfaction. "There must be a way forward." Then she was struck with revelation. Helesys reached out with her gauntlet and felt for seams in the magic, just as she'd done to escape Logath. She found dozens of them! Each a realm and through each the slightest view of what lay within—sand between her fingers, blustering mountain cold, coppery metal, the smell of ash and stench of a bog. The feelings came by smell or by touch, too quick for her to hold onto. Helesys did not know how long passed as she sifted through the realms, only that Taunauk watched in silence—as if he was seeing the same as she was, merely by watching the expressions on her face.

She was mesmerized. "The Apothecary was so close, Taunauk. She nearly strode between realms otherwise locked by death."

"Such power..." Taunauk trailed off as if he felt it taboo.

Behind her, a scream echoed through the cavern. A scream of twisted anguish that filled the space and seemed to come from everywhere. As it echoed, the sound coalesced behind them to a single spot and, in a blink, the Apothecary appeared. She dropped to her knees and then to her side, and lay crumpled on the ground.

Taunauk was already upon her, axeblade held to her shoulders. "What devilry is this?"

Helesys nearly repeated the question, then said, "Her magic is fading. So much of it was channeled into the bonfire, that when it ceased, so did her magic." Helesys said to the Apothecary, "You are lucky to return like this."

"Luck is twisted in this place," the witch said quietly, still regaining her composure. "That which should kill, does not. That which should prolong, that which should make one undying, causes a lingering death."

Taunauk asked plainly, "What should we do with her?"

Helesys wrinkled her brow. "It would be an easy thing to kill her. Probably the right thing." She sighed. "Meaningless too, in this place."

The weaver turned back to her gauntlet and to the seams of the other realms. They were fading. "We need to decide what to do with her. Our doorways are closing."

"*Your* doorways," the Apothecary gasped and struggled to her knees. "Lifetimes of work and you think you can just use my magic…" She was staring at the metal arm, as if finally realizing the edge that it gave her enemy.

"I know not from where it came," Helesys replied, "only that its abilities and insights are far beyond those of a normal mage."

The Apothecary stood on shaking legs, her beautiful lips twisted in a half-sneer. "You have upset the balance by ending the fire. You would cause thrice the undo suffering!"

Helesys regarded the witch with disdain, that which she had come to feel for nearly all powerful beings who chose not to wander the realms, who resigned themselves to withering, idle fate.

"I would cause ten times the suffering, witch, if it meant a chance for something better. If it meant a chance for this world to be free of your perversions."

"Do you mean that?" Taunauk asked quietly. "That has not been our way."

Helesys met her comrade's eyes and saw doubt in them— not doubt of purpose, but doubt of reason and morality.

"I have thought more on it," Helesys said. "Do you remember the Wode? The witch's balance is not that of the Deacon's. The Deacon asked nothing more of his villagers than would've been demanded of them were they to survive on their own. Flesh and pain from the woman's side to create a baby… No worse than the pain of childbirth and in a fraction of the time. But this realm," her eyes fell heavy upon the witch, "you have caused so much suffering and lingering deaths for personal gain. No. This will not stand."

Helesys felt the decision heavy upon her shoulders. They could not leave the witch here. Helesys had half a mind to throw her through a random portal—as if that would be any different from striking her down.

Then the roof of the cavern rumbled and a serpent's bellow echoed from high above. The goddess Irehyl plunged through the air in a mad, spiraling descent. In those fleeting moments, the feathered body and her blue Terran face looked as though they'd been plucked from a nightmare.

Taunauk backed away with a barbarian's speed. The Apothecary didn't have time to scream before the serpent crashed down on her. As quick as the goddess appeared, she twisted around and swallowed the crumpled body of the Apothecary in three horrid, crunching bites.

Helesys turned to task and pulled on the seams of the realms. They were still wide enough to pass through, but the

weaver felt that she could not choose which doorway to take—
such was the fleeting magic.

Out of the corner of her vision, Helesys saw the goddess
uncoil her great length and face the pair of them. Her eyes were
closed, just as they had been above.

"You have my gratitude," Irehyl said, her voice shaking the
cavern. "You have freed the remnants of my beloved Entae.
No longer will his bones be used for alchemy. He can be put
to rest."

Helesys could not bring herself to look back, for in that
moment, she began to doubt. They had reclaimed the bone of
Irehyl's lover… Had they been sent on a personal vendetta?

But Taunauk spoke first, "Good serpent, you are the goddess of the lost. What was Entae the god of?"

The weaver held the seams and turned to regard the goddess. Irehyl's blue face yawned and swallowed the bone of her
lover. Then her eyes opened for the first time, revealing a brilliant white light that dappled like twin gemstones.

"We were both gods of the lost," Irehyl said. "I was the
goddess of finding lost souls. Entae helped them find their way
again. Perhaps together, we can bring peace to this realm."

Helesys smiled, a fleeting gesture. The goddess's answer
was good enough. "Come, Taunauk. Let us be on our way."

The weaver flared the magic of the seams and the portal
opened, like a curtain parted to reveal a gray world beyond.
There was a new realm beyond—of this, Helesys was sure—
but they would not see until they stepped through.

The weaver and the barbarian walked through the portal,
leaving the realm awash in change and hope.

~ ~ ~

NEXT TIME ON
*A BATTLEAXE AND
A METAL ARM*
Book 7:

Ill-Fated Voyage
Available October 2021

Spoiler–Free excerpt from *BAMA 7*

What appeared at first to be a spire, was a half-buried castle. Sand dunes came up to the windows of what should have been the second or third story. Of the windows, only twisted frames and splintered fragments of glass remained. Half a dozen spires rose up behind the most prominent one, struggling to stay above the sand.

The weaver and barbarian approached cautiously; Helesys did this, not because she suspected danger, but because it felt as if walking through a graveyard. Before they reached the embankment, Helesys stopped and stared.

Throughout their journeys they had often heard of the smothering oppression of time, the withering that ground all to dust. Helesys felt as if she were staring down the proof of it, one of the omnipresent laws of the dungeon was writ small and intimate. Here was a dying thing, and some small part of Helesys wept for it.

"What is it?" Taunauk had turned and was regarding her with worry. Perhaps he thought it was a spell or something more nefarious than creeping dread.

Helesys shook her head. "It is nothing. Just poetry in the crumbling walls."

The barbarian nodded thoughtfully as if he understood her meaning, or understood enough of it. Then he turned and continued up the sandy slope, as if expecting her to come along anyway.

Helesys knew then that there were things here which she could not reconcile: She could not face realm after realm and certain, uncountable deaths, not while staring at a crumbling castle, a trapped god, or a forgotten civilization. She could do nothing, except continue forward—lest she be ground to dust and buried like all the rest.

They climbed the sand and up through a broken window, which was nearly two stories tall itself. The inside was covered in sand, turning what might've been a towering five story grand hall into one merely a story or two high, and where the rafters were close enough to touch but otherwise unbroken. Boxes, blankets and bottles littered the sand. At first glance, the arrangement looked haphazard—but blankets were piled near boxes and bottles were half-filled with water and positioned away from the scant rays of sunlight that filtered through the cracks in the roof. A single shield hung from the rafters on the left wall like a trophy. Its face was silver, plain and polished to a high sheen so that it gleamed, even in the faint light. Then Taunauk pointed to the far wall, to another dune entrance and tracks in the sand.

To be continued October 2021

Thank you for Reading

I hope you enjoyed reading this story as much as I enjoyed writing it.

If you did, I would massively appreciate a short review on Amazon or your favorite book website. Reviews are crucial for any author, and a starred review or even just a line or two can make a huge difference.

It's especially true for the start of a series. Thanks and I hope you enjoy the next one!

Looking for more Engrossing Fantasy?

You might like **Tales from Another World,** an ongoing short story series containing stories about sorcerers, druids, mortals, gods, thieves, and all other manner of Terrans.

The 2nd installment is out and it may or may not have ties to the world of *A Battleaxe and a Metal Arm.* So, if you're looking for more engrossing fantasy stories, read on and see how deep the rabbit hole goes.

What questions do you have about *A Battleaxe and a Metal Arm*?

If you've read this far, hopefully you'll read a bit further—both in this book and across the series. I'm not sure how most authors write serials and how much of it is flying by the seat of their pants, but that's not how I do things. For all the major questions that might come up in BAMA, I already have answers for 95% of them. Same goes for the major plot points, twists and climaxes. That might sound boring to some, especially some of you other authors who enjoy variations of writing into the dark, but I think having a solid blueprint is paramount to writing a long series.

So, what questions do you have about the story? Here are a few:

1) ~~What is the dungeon?~~ It's a soul trap of overwhelming size and power. But where did it come from? Is it a force of nature or an ill-made weapon, or perhaps something else entirely?

2) Who were Helesys and Taunauk before they got trapped? At this point, we know little more than their names and abilities. How well did they know each other beforehand?

3) How did Helesys get her metal arm?

4) Who is Shawn? Why does he feel so familiar to Helesys and Taunauk?

5) Who is the Wolf King and what sinister plans does he have for our heroes? How did he come to rule over the Dungeon? How does the Gatekeeper factor into all this?

Did I miss any questions? Probably. Connect with me and other *BAMA* fans on social media and compare questions!

I've got plans. I've got answers. And I've got them on a drip-feed. Keep reading and expect to find out a little more to the mysteries with each installment. Hopefully, you're as excited about this series as I am.

Connect with the Author

If you want to stay up to date on the latest about Samuel's publishing news and blog, check out his website and consider signing up for his monthly newsletter.

www.SamuelFlemingBooks.com

Samuel can also be found on Reddit, Goodreads and Facebook.

Samuel Fleming is a Science Fiction and Fantasy author.

He grew up in Maryland, spending most of his time swimming and writing. Swimming gave him a lot of time to daydream, so the two hobbies complemented each other well. Idle day dreams turned into stories, some of which stuck with him for years. These days he swims a little less and writes a lot more.

He loves a good story no matter the medium: Books, TV, video games, comics, tabletop RPG's, or podcasts—most of which he attempts to share with his wife and three kids, and occasionally on his blog.

www.ingramcontent.com/pod-product-compliance
Lightning Source LLC
Chambersburg PA
CBHW030648190726
48286CB00008B/2717